MARK
DAWSON

GHOSTS

WELBECK

First published in 2023 by Welbeck Fiction Limited,
an imprint of Welbeck Publishing Group
Offices in: London – 20 Mortimer Street, London W1T 3JW &
Sydney – Level 17, 207 Kent St, Sydney NSW 2000 Australia
www.welbeckpublishing.com

First published in 2014
This edition published by Welbeck Fiction Limited, part of
Welbeck Publishing Group, in 2023

A CIP catalogue record for this book is available from the British Library

Hardback ISBN: 978-1-78739-764-4
Trade paperback ISBN: 978-1-78739-765-1

Printed and bound by CPI Group (UK) Ltd., Croydon, CR0 4YY

FSC
www.fsc.org
MIX
Paper | Supporting
responsible forestry
FSC® C171272

10 9 8 7 6 5 4 3 2 1

GHOSTS

For my family

PART 1
LONDON – EIGHT YEARS AGO

1

The van was parked at the side of the road. It was a white Renault and it had been prepared to look just like one of the maintenance vehicles that Virgin Media used. It was parked at the junction of Upper Ground and Rennie Street. The spot had been chosen carefully; it allowed an excellent view of the entrance to the Oxo Tower brasserie on London's South Bank. The interior of the van had been prepared carefully, too. A console had been installed along the right-hand side of the vehicle, with monitors displaying the feed from the low light colour camera that was fitted to the roof. There was a 360-degree periscope that could be raised and lowered as appropriate, various recording devices, a dual-band radio antenna and a microwave receiver. It was a little cramped in the back for the two men inside.

The intelligence officer using the equipment had quickly become oblivious to any discomfort. He reached across to the console and selected a different video feed; they had installed a piggyback into the embassy's security system two weeks ago and now he had access to all those separate feeds, as well as to an array of exterior cameras they had also hijacked. The monitor flickered and then displayed the footage from the security camera that surveyed the building. He could see the big Mercedes S280 that the chauffeur had parked there, but, apart from that, there was nothing.

The second man was sitting just to the side of the technician, watching the action over his shoulder. This man was anxious, and he knew that it was radiating from him.

'Change views,' he said tensely. 'Back inside.'

The technician did as he was told and discarded the view for another one from inside the restaurant. The targets were still in the main room, finishing their desserts. The first target was facing away from the camera, but she was still recognisable. The second target was toying with an unlit cigarette, turning it between his fingers. The second man looked at the footage. It looked as if the meal was finally coming to an end. The two targets would be leaving soon.

'Group,' the second man said into the headset microphone. 'This is Control. Comms check.'

'Copy that, Control, this is One. Strength ten.'

'Eight, also strength ten.'

'Twelve, copy that.'

'Ten, strength ten.'

'Eleven, same here. Strength ten.'

'Five. Ditto for me.'

'Eleven, what can you see?'

The agent code-named Eleven was standing at the bar, enjoying a drink as he waited for a table. His name was Duffy and he had latterly been in the Royal Marines. Control could see him in the footage from the camera and watched as he angled himself away from the couple and put his hand up to his mouth.

'They're finishing,' he said, his voice clipped and quiet as he spoke into the discreet microphone slipped beneath the strap of his watch. 'The waiter just asked if they wanted coffees and they didn't. Won't be long.'

Satisfied, Control sat back and watched. Very few people knew his given name. He was dressed well, as was his habit, in a pale blue shirt and tastefully spotted braces. He held his glasses in his right hand, absently tapping one of the arms against his lips. He had been in day-to-day command of Group Fifteen since its inception, but, these days, he rarely oversaw operations personally. He was a desk man now. He preferred to pull the strings, the dark hand in the shadows. The puppet master. But this operation was personal and he wanted to be closer to the action. He would have preferred to smell the gun smoke, if that had been possible. He would have preferred to pull the trigger.

Watching would be an acceptable substitute.

It was an expensive and exclusive restaurant. The wall facing the river was one huge expanse of glass, with doors leading out onto a terrace. The views were outstanding and Control knew, from several meals there himself, that the food was just as good.

The bright sunlight refracted against the watch that the first target wore on her wrist and the diamond earrings that must have cost her a small fortune. Control watched and felt his temper slowly curdle. He had been introduced to her by a mutual Iranian friend. The name she had given him was Alexandra Kyznetsov. He knew now that that was not her name. Her real name was Anastasia Ivanovna Semenko and, instead of being a businesswoman with interests in the chemical industry, she was an agent in the pay of the Russian Federal Security Service. She was in her early forties, but she had invested heavily in cosmetic surgery and, as a result, she could have passed for a woman fifteen years younger. Control had found her attractive and he had enjoyed her flirtatious manner on the occasions that they had met.

Now, though, that just made her betrayal *worse*.

Control stared at the screen and contemplated the frantic action of the last three days. That was how long he'd had to plan the operation. Three days. It was hopelessly insufficient, especially for something as delicate as this, but the role that Semenko played cast her as something of a globetrotter and it was difficult to find a reliable itinerary for her; she tended to change it on a whim. She had only just returned from business in Saudi Arabia. Control had only green-lit the operation when it was confirmed that she was stopping in London before returning to Moscow. The team had then been assembled and briefed. Control had considered the precise detail of the plan and, by and large, he was satisfied with it. It was as good as he would be able to manage in the limited time that he had available.

The second target laughed at something that Semenko said. Control switched his attention to him. He had introduced himself as Andrei Dragunov, but, again, that was a lie. His real name was Pascha Shcherbatov. He, too, was Russian, a long-time KGB agent and an intelligence man to the quick; since the fall of the Wall, he had amassed considerable influence in the SVR, the successor to his notorious previous employer, and was now considered to be something of an operator. A worthy opponent, certainly.

Semenko clasped the hand of the maitre d', her face beaming. Both targets got up, leaving money on the table, and made for the archway that opened into the lobby.

'DOLLAR and SNOW are on the move,' Control reported. 'Stand ready.'

Shcherbatov's phone rang and he stopped, putting it to his ear. Semenko paused, waiting for him. Control stared at the pirated feed, willing himself to read Shcherbatov's lips, but it was hopeless: the angle was wrong and the quality of the image was too poor. He watched, frowning hard. Shcherbatov smiled broadly, replaced the phone and spoke with Semenko. Control hoped that their plans had not changed. That would throw things into confusion.

'Control to One and Twelve,' Control said into the mike. 'They are on the move.'

'One, Control. Copy that.'

Control watched as Semenko and Shcherbatov headed towards the exit. The pair stepped beneath the camera and out of shot. 'Keep on them,' Control said, and the technician tapped out a command and switched views to a new camera. This one was in the lift and, as he watched, the doors opened and the two of them stepped inside. Shcherbatov pressed the button for the ground floor. The camera juddered as the lift began to descend. 'Targets are in the lift,' Control reported. 'One and Twelve, stand ready.'

'One, Control. Copy that.'

The technician swung around on his chair and brought up another feed on the second monitor. It offered a wide-angle view of the street outside the restaurant. Control could see Semenko's chauffeur. He was a large man, powerfully built, with a balding head. They knew he had a background in the Spetsnaz and would certainly be armed. He wore a pair of frameless glasses and was dressed in a dark suit and open-necked shirt. Control watched as he stepped out of the shadows, tossing a cigarette to the floor and stomping it out.

The lift came to a stop and the door opened.

Semenko emerged into the wide shot first, walking with a confident bounce across the space to the Mercedes. Shcherbatov followed, his phone pressed to his ear again. The chauffeur opened the rear door for his passengers and, as they slipped inside, he opened the front door and got in himself.

He started the engine. Control could see the fumes rising from the exhaust.

The Mercedes reversed and turned and then pulled away, moving quickly.

'Targets are in play,' Control reported.

2

Beatrix Rose was sitting astride a Kawasaki motorcycle on Rennie Street. The visor of her helmet was up and the cool air was fresh against her face. The usual buzz of adrenaline had kicked in as the operation moved into its final phase. She was a professional with years of experience behind her; too professional to let excitement render her less useful than she would need to be.

She listened to the comms chatter in the receiver that was pressed into her ear, the detailed commentary as the Mercedes passed from the back of the restaurant and onto Upper Ground. She had memorised this part of London, at first with the aid of a map and then, over the course of the morning, three hours of careful reconnaissance that had fixed the local geography in her mind. She was confident that she was as prepared as she could be.

'*They're turning east towards the Bridge,*' intoned Control.

There was another motorcycle next to her. The agent sitting astride it was nervous, despite the time he had spent in the army and then the SAS. He had a glittering résumé, with one mission behind the lines during the second Iraq War a particular standout, but it was one thing to go into battle during a war, when the rules of engagement were clear, and quite another to conduct a clandestine extrajudicial operation like this, with no backup or recognition, and the likelihood of incarceration, or worse, if things went wrong. The man had his visor open, like she did, but where she was clear-eyed and focused, he looked ashen.

'Milton,' she called across to him.

He didn't respond.

'*Milton.*'

He turned to face her.

'You all right?'

'Fine,' he called back.

'You look like you're going to be sick.'

'I'm fine.'

'Remember your training. You've done more difficult things than this.'

He nodded.

Beatrix Rose was Number One, the most senior agent in the Group. The man on the second bike was John Milton. He was Number Twelve. The Group was a small and highly select team. Twelve members. Milton was its most junior member and his presence in it was at least partly because of her influence.

The previous Number Twelve, a cantankerous Irishman who had served with the Special Boat Service before being transferred, had been killed in a firefight with al-Qaeda sympathisers in Yemen three months earlier. Control had identified ten potential replacements to fill his spot on the team and had deputed the job of selecting the most promising soldier to her. She had interviewed all of them and then personally oversaw the selection weekend when their number had gradually been whittled down, one at a time, until Milton had been the last man standing.

Beatrix had known before the weekend had started that it was going to end up that way. His commanding officers described him as a brilliant soldier who was brave and selfless. They also spoke of a steely determination and a relentless focus on the goal at hand. He did not allow anything to stand in his way. He had demonstrated all of that. He was the most promising recruit that she had ever worked with and, in all the time that she had been Number One, she had tutored two men and two women who had replaced fallen team members. There had been more than three hundred possible recruits for those four spots and Milton was better than all of them. His inclusion in this operation was part of his ongoing operational development. During an operative's first year of service as Twelve, ad hoc active deployments were included at Control's direction. These complemented the elite training programme provided by the Manor House – the training facility in Wiltshire.

'Here they come,' she called out.

The Mercedes turned the corner and headed in their direction. Beatrix flipped her visor down and gave the engine a twist of revs. Milton did the same, gunning the engine and then, as the Mercedes moved past them, closing his visor and pulling out into the empty road.

'One, Control,' Beatrix said.

'Go ahead, One.'

'We're in pursuit.'

3

'Control, One. Roger that.'

Control had placed his agents carefully: One and Twelve east of the restaurant on Rennie Street; Five and Eight in a second van, currently idling in Southwark Street; Ten on a third bike, waiting on Stamford Street in the event that they went west instead of east; Eleven inside the restaurant. He was confident that they had all eventualities covered.

The driver of the surveillance van started the engine and they pulled out into the traffic and headed north. The Mercedes was out of sight, but One was providing a commentary on its movements and it was a simple thing to follow.

Control twisted the wedding ring on his left hand. Despite his satisfaction with their preparation, he was still nervous. This had to be perfect. The operation was totally off the book; usually, the files with the details of their targets were passed down to him by either MI5 or MI6, but that wasn't the case this time. Neither agency had sanctioned this operation and he would have even less cover than he usually did if anything went wrong. It wasn't just that this was unofficial business – all of the work they did was unofficial – it was personal.

None of his agents knew that. He had deceived them.

'Control, One. Report.'

'Target is waiting at the junction at Blackfriars Bridge.'

Control knew their itinerary for the rest of the day. Semenko and Shcherbatov were going to a meeting.

As far as they knew, the meeting was with him.

It was an appointment that Control had no intention of keeping.

4

The Mercedes picked up speed as it turned onto Blackfriars Bridge. It found a small gap in the traffic. Beatrix opened the throttle in response, keeping the Mercedes a few car lengths ahead of them. Their intelligence suggested that the woman she knew as DOLLAR had an appointment with a contact on Victoria Embankment; it looked as if the intelligence would prove to be accurate.

Beatrix stayed between fifty and a hundred yards behind the car; Milton was another twenty yards behind her. She kept up a running commentary as they gradually worked their way south-east, towards the river. 'North end of the Bridge, turning off ... onto the Embankment, heading west ... passing Blackfriars Pier ... coming up to Waterloo Bridge, following the river to the south.'

The traffic started to queue as they reached Victoria Embankment Gardens. Beatrix bled away almost all the speed, ducking in behind a bus that was idling opposite Cleopatra's Needle. She could see the Mercedes through the windows of the bus and, beyond it, the Houses of Parliament.

'One, Control. Waiting at the lights at Embankment Pier.'

'Acknowledged,' said Control. *'They'll continue south.'*

'Copy that.' The lights changed, the traffic started to move, the last pedestrians broke into self-conscious trots as they hurried out of the way. 'He's accelerating towards Hungerford Bridge.'

She gunned the engine and sped forwards, not about to get stuck should the lights turn against her.

Control's voice crackled again: *'Control, Group. This is as good a spot as any. Five?'*

'In position,' reported Number Five. *'One and Twelve. Get ready. Here we come.'*

Beatrix watched: a white van, not dissimilar to the one in which Control was watching, had been running parallel to them on Whitehall. Now, though, it jerked out into the traffic from Richmond Terrace and blocked the road in front of the Mercedes. Number Eight – Oliver Spenser – was at the wheel. Number Five – Lydia Chisolm – was alongside him. Both agents were armed with SA80 machine guns, but the plan did not anticipate that they would need to use them.

Beatrix braked to thirty and then twenty. 'One, Control. They're stopping.'

'Control, One and Twelve. You have authorisation. Take them out.'

Beatrix rolled the bike carefully between the waiting cars: a red Peugeot, a dirty grey Volvo, an open double-decker bus that had been fitted out for guided tours. The Mercedes was ahead of the bus, blocked in between it and the delivery van in front. Beatrix reached the car, coming to a halt and bracing the heavy weight of the bike with her right leg. Milton rolled up behind her. Neither of them spoke; they didn't need to, they were operating purely on instinct by this stage, implementing the plan. Beatrix quickly scoped the immediate location: the inside lane was temporarily clear to the left of the Mercedes, the pavement beyond that was empty and then it was the wide-open stretch of the Thames. No need to concern themselves with catching civilians in the crossfire.

Beatrix released her grip on the handlebars and unzipped her leather jacket. She was wearing a strap around her shoulder and a Heckler & Koch UMP was attached to it. She raised the machine pistol, steadied it with her left hand around the foregrip, aimed at the Mercedes and squeezed the trigger.

The window shattered, shards spilling out onto the road like handfuls of diamonds.

Milton was supposed to be doing the same, but he had stopped.

Beatrix noticed but didn't have time to direct him. She was completely professional. Even as the machine pistol jerked and spat in her hand, her aim was such that every round passed into the cabin of the car. The gun chewed through all thirty rounds in the detachable magazine, spraying lead through the window.

The driver somehow managed to get the Mercedes into gear and it jerked forwards. He must have been hit because he couldn't control the car, slaloming it against the delivery van, bouncing across the road, slicing through the inside lane and then fishtailing. It slid through one hundred and eighty degrees and then wedged itself between a tree and a street lamp. The horn sounded, a long and uninterrupted note. The car had only travelled twenty feet, but Beatrix couldn't see into it any longer.

'Milton!'

She was fresh out of ammunition and he was the nearest.

'Milton! Move!'

He was still on the bike, frozen.

The passenger side door opened and SNOW fell out. The car's wild manoeuvre meant that the body of the car was now between Beatrix and him; SNOW ducked down beneath the wing, out of sight.

'Milton! SNOW is running.'

'I've got it,' Milton said, but she could hear the uncertainty in his voice.

He was corpsing; Beatrix had not anticipated that.

She ejected the dry magazine and slapped in another, watching through the corner of her eye as he got off the Kawasaki and drew his own UMP.

Beatrix put the kickstand down. There was a terrific clamour all about: the Mercedes' horn was still sounding, tourists on the bus – with a clear view of what had just happened – were screaming in fright as they clambered to the back of the deck, and, in the distance, there came the ululation of a siren.

Too soon, surely? Perhaps, but it was a timely reminder; the plan only allowed them a few seconds before they needed to effect their escapes.

Beatrix approached the car, her gun extended and unwavering.

It was carnage. The driver was slumped forwards, blood splashed against the jagged shards of windscreen that were still held within the frame. The full weight of his chest was pressed up against the wheel, sounding the horn. DOLLAR was leaning against the side of the car, a track of entry wounds stitching up from her shoulder into her neck and then into the side of her head. Her hair was matted with blood and brain.

Beatrix strode up to the car and fired two short bursts: one for the driver and one for DOLLAR. She kept moving forward, the machine pistol smoking as she held it ahead of her, zoning out the noise behind her but acutely aware of the timer counting down in her head. The man and the woman were unmoving. She looked through the driver's side window and saw a briefcase on the passenger seat. They were not tasked with recovering intelligence, but it was hardwired into her from a hundred similar missions and so she quickly ran around to the passenger door, opened it and collected it.

'*Control, One,*' came the barked voice in her earpiece. '*Report.*'

'The driver and DOLLAR are down.'

'*What about SNOW?*'

'He's running.'

There was panic in his reply: '*What?*'

'I repeat, SNOW is on foot. Twelve is pursuing.'

5

Milton left the bike behind him and sprinted. SNOW was already fifty feet ahead, adjacent to the Battle of Britain memorial. The great wheel of the London Eye was on the other side of the river and, ahead, a line of touring coaches had been slotted into the bays next to the pavement.

The target dodged through the line of stalled traffic; nothing was able to move with the shot-up Mercedes blocking the road ahead. He turned his head, stumbling a little as he did, saw Milton in pursuit and sprinted harder. He was older than Milton, but he had obviously kept himself in good shape; he maintained a steady pace, driven on by fear. Milton's motorcycle leathers were not made for running and the helmet he was wearing – he dared not remove it for fear of identifying himself – limited his field of vision.

He took out his Sig and fired a shot. It was wild, high and wide and shattered the windscreen of one of the big parked coaches. It inspired SNOW to find another burst of pace, cutting between two of the parked buses. Milton lost sight of him. He ran between a truck and the car in front of it, passed between the two buses behind the ones that his quarry had used and saw him again. A second shot was prevented by a red telephone box and then a tall ash tree.

Milton heard the up-and-down wail of a police siren. It sounded as if it was on the Embankment, behind him, closing the distance.

Milton stopped, dropped to one knee and brought up the Sig. He breathed in and out, trying to steady his aim, and, for a moment, he had a clear shot. He used his left hand to swipe up his visor, breathed again, deep and easy, and started to squeeze the trigger.

SNOW ploughed into the middle of a group of tourists.

Shit.

Milton dropped his arm; there was no shot.

He closed the visor and ran onwards, just as he saw the target again: he had clambered onto the wall that separated the pavement from the river and, with a final defiant look back in his direction, he leapt into space and plunged into the water.

Milton zigzagged through the panicking tourists until he was at the wall and looked down into the greeny-black waters. There was nothing for a moment and then, already thirty feet distant, he saw SNOW bob to the surface. The currents were notoriously strong at this part of the river. The rip tides were powerful enough to swallow even the strongest swimmer, but SNOW was not fighting and the water swept him away, quickly out of range.

The siren was louder now, and, as Milton turned to face it, he saw that the patrol car was less than a hundred feet away, working its way around the stalled queue.

Milton paused, caught between running and standing still. He froze. He didn't know what to do.

'*Milton,*' came Number One's voice in his ear.

He turned to his left. Beatrix was on the pavement, between the river and the row of buses, gunning her Kawasaki hard. Milton pushed the Sig back into its holster and zipped up his jacket. Beatrix braked, the rear wheel bouncing up a few inches, then slamming back down again. Milton got onto the back; Beatrix had a slight figure and he looped his left arm around her waist and fixed his right hand to grip the rear of the pillion seat. Milton was six foot tall and heavy with muscle, but the bike had a 998cc four-cylinder engine and his extra weight was as nothing.

It jerked forward hungrily as Beatrix revved it and released her grip on the brakes.

6

Beatrix looked out of the window of Control's office. It was the evening, two hours after the operation. It was a habit to debrief as soon as possible after the work had been done and, usually, those were not difficult meetings. Normally, the operations passed off exactly as they were planned. They were not botched like this one had been.

Control was busying himself with the tray that his assistant, Captain Tanner, had brought in; it held a teapot, two cups, a jug of milk and a bowl of sugar cubes. He poured out two cups. Beatrix could see that he was angry. His face was drawn and pale, the muscles in his cheeks twitching. He had said very little to her, but she knew him well enough to know that the recriminations were coming. The crockery chimed as he rattled the spoon against it, stirring in his sugar. He brought the cups across the room, depositing one on her side of his desk and taking the other one around to sip at it as he stood at the window.

'So?' he began.

'Sir?'

'What happened?'

Beatrix had known, of course, that the question was coming. The mission had been an unmitigated failure. The watchword of the Group was discretion, and the shooting had been the first item on the news and the papers were leading with a variation of the same picture: Milton, in black leathers and a helmet with a mirrored visor, his arm extended as he aimed at the fleeing SNOW, his abandoned motorcycle in the background. The headline in the *Times* was typical: MURDER ON THE STREETS OF LONDON.

'It was just bad luck,' she said.

'Luck? We plan so that luck isn't a factor, Number One. Luck has *nothing* to do with it.'

'The driver managed to get the car away from us. That was just bad luck.'

'It was Twelve's responsibility to neutralise the driver. Are you saying it was his fault?'

Beatrix had given thought to what she should say. The honest thing to do would be to throw Milton under the bus. This had been his first examination and he had flunked it. He had frozen at the critical moment. They had the targets cold, helpless, and it had been his corpsing that had given SNOW the opportunity to make a run for it. And even then, she knew Milton was a good enough shot to have taken him down.

She could have said all of that and it would have been true. She could have burned him, but it wouldn't have been the right thing to do.

She had some empathy. She remembered her own introduction to the Group. The operation when she had lost her own cherry had been a fuck-up, too; not quite like this, but then she had been in Iraq and not on the streets of London, far from prying eyes and the possibility of your mistakes being amplified by a media that couldn't get enough of something so audacious and dramatic.

Her own wobble had been between her, the female agent who had been Number Six in those days and her victim, an Iraqi official who was passing information to the insurgency; Beatrix had paused at the moment of truth and that meant that the man she had just stabbed in the gut had been able to punch her in the face, freeing himself for long enough to hobble into the busy street outside. Number Six had pursued him outside and fired two shots into his head and then, keeping bystanders away with the threat of the gun, she had hijacked a car and driven them both away. Beatrix remembered how Control had asked her how it had gone. Six had covered for her, telling him that the operation had passed off without incident and that it had all been straightforward. Beatrix would have been cashiered without hesitation if Six had told Control the truth. So she understood what had happened to Milton. It did not diminish her opinion of him. It did not make her question her decision to recommend him.

'It wasn't his fault,' Beatrix told Control, looking him straight in the eye. 'He did his job, just as we planned it.'

'So you say. But he went in pursuit of SNOW?'

'Yes.'

'And?'

'He never had a clear shot, not one he could take without a significant risk that he would hit a bystander. The rules of engagement were clear. This had to be at no risk.'

'I know what the bloody rules of engagement were, Number One,' he said sharply. 'I wrote them.'

'If you want to blame anyone, blame me.'

Control flustered and, for a moment, Beatrix was convinced that he *was* going to blame her. That would have been all right. She had been a member of the Group for six years and that was already pushing at the top end of an agent's average life expectancy. It wasn't an assignment that you kept if you had something to lose. Beatrix had a daughter and a husband and a family life that she enjoyed more than she had ever expected. She had done her time and she had done it well, but all things had to come to an end eventually. She wouldn't have resisted if he blamed her and busted her out of the Group. There would be something else for her, something safer, something where getting shot at was not something she would come to expect.

But he didn't blame her.

'It's a bloody mess,' he said instead, sighing with impatience. 'A bloody, *bloody* mess. The police have been told it's an underworld thing. They'll buy that, if only because the prospect of their own government sanctioning a hit is too bloody ludicrous to credit.'

'The only thing we left was Milton's bike, and that's clean. There's no way back to us from that.'

'You're sure?'

'Absolutely sure.'

He took his saucer and cup to his desk and sat down. He exhaled deeply.

'What a mess,' he said again. He was frustrated, and that was to be expected, but the immediate threat of the explosion of his temper had passed. 'Where is Milton now?'

'Training,' she told him.

That was true. He had barely left the quarters where the Group's logistics were based since the operation. The range-master said that he had been on the range with a target pistol, firing over and over until the targets were torn to shreds, then loading another target and pushing it further out and doing it all again.

'Are you still sure about him?'

'He'll be fine,' Beatrix said. 'When have I ever been wrong about a recruit?'

'I know,' Control said, leaning back. 'Never.'

He exhaled again and sipped at his tea.

Beatrix looked beyond him, beyond the plush interior of his office where so many death warrants were signed, and out into the darkness. London was going about its business, just as usual. Beatrix's eyes narrowed their focus until she noticed the image in the glass: the back of Control's head and, facing him, her own reflection. She stood at a cross-roads, with a choice of how to proceed: she could say nothing, and go back to her family, or she could do what she had decided she had to do and begin a conversation that could very easily become difficult.

'There was one more thing,' she said.

'What?'

'I pulled some evidence out of the car.'

Control sat forward. 'That wasn't in the plan.'

'I know. Force of habit, I suppose. It was there, I took it.'

'And?'

'And you should probably take a look.'

She had travelled to the office on her own motorbike and had stowed the case in a rucksack. She opened the drawstring, took it out and laid it on Control's desk. The case had been locked and she had unscrewed the hinges to get it open; it was held together by one of her husband's belts at the moment. Beatrix unhooked it and removed the top half of the case. There was a clear plastic bag with six flash drives and, beneath that, a manilla envelope. Inside the envelope was a thick sheaf of photographs. They were printed on glossy five-by-eight paper and had been taken by someone from a high vantage point, using a powerful telephoto lens. It was a series, with two people in shot. The first person was a man. He was wearing a heavy overcoat and a woollen hat had been pulled down over his ears. The picture had been taken in a park during the winter; the trees in the foreground were bare and a pile of slush, perhaps from a melted snowman, was visible fifty feet away. The man was bent down, standing over a park bench. There was a woman on the bench.

Despite the distance and the angle that the picture had been taken, it was still obvious that the standing man was Control.

'What is this?' he asked brusquely.

'It was in the case . . .'

'Yes,' he snapped. 'You said. I have no idea why.'

'That's you, sir, isn't it?'

'If you say so.'

The atmosphere had become uncomfortable, but Beatrix couldn't draw back.

'The woman on the bench . . .'

Control made a show of examining the photograph more closely.

'It's DOLLAR,' Beatrix said.

He said nothing.

'I don't understand, sir . . .'

'Your job is not to understand, Number One. Your job is to follow the orders that I give you.'

He paused; Beatrix thought he was hesitating, searching for the words to say what he wanted to say, but he didn't say anything else. He just stared at her instead.

'Sir?'

He indicated the flash drives with a dismissive downward brush of his hand. 'Have you looked at these?'

'No, sir,' she said, although that was a lie.

'Very good.' He shuffled in his chair, straightening his shoulders. 'I want you to keep a close eye on Milton. It might be that we were wrong about him – and we can't afford passengers. If we were wrong, we'll need to reassign him. Understood?'

She nodded that she did.

'That will be all for now. You're dismissed, Number One.'

Beatrix stood, still uncomfortable and confused, and then turned for the door.

She was halfway across the room before Control cleared his throat.

'Look, Number One . . . Beatrix. Please, sit down again.'

She turned back and did so. Control had come around the desk and now he was standing by the mantelpiece.

'You're right. I did meet her. A couple of times. Looks like she decided she'd like some pictures to mark the occasion. I can't tell you why we met and I can't tell you what we spoke about, save to say that it was connected to the operation. The details are classified. All you need to know, Beatrix, is that you were given a file with her name on it. And you know what that means.'

'I do, sir. Termination.'

'That's right. Is there anything else you want to ask me?'

She looked at him: a little portly, a little soft, his frame belying his years of service in MI6, including, she knew, years behind the Iron Curtain during the Cold War and a distinguished campaign in the Falklands. He was looking at her with an expression of seeming concern, but, beneath that, she saw a foundation of suspicion and caution.

Beatrix was a professional assassin, Number One amidst a collection of twelve of the most dangerous men and women in the employ of Her Majesty. She was responsible for the deaths of over eighty people all around the world. Bad people who had done bad things. She was not afraid of very much. But Control was not the sort of man you would ever want to cross. She looked at him again, regarding her with shrew-like curiosity, and she was frightened.

The thought began to form that she had just made a very, very bad mistake.

7

Beatrix had a house in a pleasant area of East London. There were estates surrounding it on all sides, but the grid of streets that included Lavender Grove was a peaceful and safe middle-class enclave that was, she thought, a good place to set up home. The house that she and her husband had bought five years earlier was a three-bedroom terrace, slotted between properties owned by a kindly retired couple and a young banker who was often abroad. The front of the house had a narrow strip of garden that was separated from the pavement by a set of iron railings and they had fixed colourful hanging baskets on either side of the brightly painted red front door. There was a larger garden to the rear, long and narrow, just big enough for the chickens that Beatrix had always wanted. It was a warm house with plenty of space for her, her husband and their daughter.

They were talking about adopting another child and the house would be big enough for him or her, too, although it would be a little tight. It just needed to get them through the next eighteen months. Beatrix had decided that she would request reassignment from the Group after that; she had been doing it more than long enough. You could reduce the risks involved with an assignment with excellent planning, and Beatrix was fastidious about that, but there was always the chance that something might go wrong: bad intelligence, something that could not have been predicted, a lucky shot. Look at what had happened. She had been tempting fate for years and she knew very well that, eventually, that would catch up with her. She was going to get out before that could happen.

She slotted the bike into the nearest space to the house and killed the engine. She took off her helmet, angled her head and looked at her reflection in the mirror. She looked fine: the ride across London had given her some time to think and, now that she had taken a moment to consider it, she wondered whether she might have been overreacting to her conversation with Control. There was probably a very good explanation for the meeting he had taken with DOLLAR, whoever she was. It was entirely possible that he had been gathering intelligence, prior to green-lighting the operation to eliminate her. Yes, there would be an explanation for it all, but right now, Beatrix wanted to switch off.

It was a pleasant day, unseasonably warm, and Beatrix was in a good mood as she crossed the pavement, opened the gate and then the front door.

'I'm home,' she called out.

There was no answer.

That was strange. Her husband, Lucas, was a web developer and he worked from the second bedroom upstairs. It was past four o'clock as well, and so their daughter, Isabella, should have been home from nursery.

Beatrix took off her jacket and hung it up. Perhaps they had gone to play in the park. She unfastened the clasps of her shoulder holster and took it off. She unclipped the leather strap that held the Sig Sauer in place, withdrew it and popped out the magazine. She laid the gun and the magazine on the table. She had a gun safe upstairs and would put them away just as soon as she had poured herself a glass of water.

She went through into the kitchen. There was a pile of unopened post on the counter. She flipped through with idle interest: bills, junk mail, nothing interesting.

She took the glass of water into the sitting room.

She dropped the glass.

Lucas was sitting on the sofa. Isabella was next to him. He had his arm around the girl's shoulders.

Number Five was sitting in the armchair facing them, a silenced semi-automatic laid across her lap.

Number Eight was standing by the door to the hallway, a silenced semi-automatic in his right hand, aimed at her.

Beatrix built a quick mental picture of possible weapons that were within reach: the letter opener on the sideboard; the paperweight next to it; a series of books in the bookcase, some of them hardback, some of them reasonably heavy; the switchblade in her right front pocket; the glass bowl that they used to hold fruit.

She was suddenly rabbit-punched in the kidneys; a sharp pain blossomed through her chest all the way down to her diaphragm. She stumbled forwards a step, bracing herself on the sideboard, before strong hands gripped her around the shoulders and spun her around. She glimpsed the cruel face of a third agent, Number Ten, as he drew back his head and then butted her in the nose. She dropped down onto her backside, blood over her face.

Beatrix got to her hands and knees.

Ten kicked her in the ribs and she thudded into the sideboard again, sweeping her arm across the surface so that the lamp toppled over and the letter opener fell between the furniture and the wall. She lay flat, her hand inches away from it; it was too far away to get it without being noticed.

Kick me again.

Beatrix raised herself up again and Ten booted her in the ribs for a second time. She landed against the sideboard, reached beneath it for the letter opener and palmed it, reversing it and sliding the blade up into her sleeve.

'That's enough,' Five said.

Beatrix bore her weight on one arm and pushed up.

'You're going to play ball, right, Beatrix?'

She wiped away the blood.

'Because, you know, it'll be so much better if you do. I don't want to have to murder you in front of your family.'

She looked up. Her husband looked back at her with pained, confused eyes. He didn't know what she really did for a living; he thought that she was still in the military.

Beatrix felt a pit opening in her stomach and, for a brief moment, the strength drained from her legs.

She mastered it quickly.

'I'm going to play ball,' she replied.

'That's right. Are you armed?'

'No.'

'So where's your weapon?'

'Outside. In the hall.'

'Any others in the house?'

'No.'

'All right. Get up.'

She did as she was told and stood. She moved gingerly, her ribs blaring with pain; it felt like a couple were broken.

Beatrix looked through the window as another two agents walked down the front path. Number Nine and Number Eleven.

Five, Eight, Nine, Ten and Eleven.

Beatrix knew them all.

Five's name was Lydia Chisholm. She had joined the group after a career in the Special Reconnaissance Regiment. Its agents operated in plainclothes, often submerged in deep cover, and it employed a unit of forty women dubbed 'the Amazons' by a lazy and unoriginal commanding officer. Five had been the pick of the bunch. She was tall and broad and muscular and Beatrix knew that her record had been excellent since she had transferred, with a series of flawlessly executed kills.

Eight was Oliver Spenser. Beatrix had supervised his training. He had demonstrated a lack of control and a propensity to aggression and she had recommended against his selection; Control had overruled her. His Special Boat Service background was more traditional for the Group. He was more of a blunt weapon; if Five was a knife, Eight was a cudgel. Both were dangerous.

Ten, the agent who had knocked her to the ground, was Joshua Joyce. Nine and Eleven, the agents who were just letting themselves into the house, were Connor English and Bryan Duffy. All three were SAS.

'What do you want?' Beatrix asked.

'You need to come with us,' Five said calmly.

'Fine,' Beatrix said. 'There's no need for this to be messy.'

'I agree. No need at all.'

Beatrix had no intention of going with them and it most certainly *was* going to be messy. She would have gladly sacrificed herself for the lives of her husband and child, but she knew, for sure, that there was no outcome that she could negotiate that would not end with her family being shot.

She heard Ten shuffle his feet. Three or four feet behind her.

She felt the cold metal of the letter opener as she held it against the inside of her wrist.

'Control doesn't trust me?'

'He wants to be sure that he can.'

She could guess what their preferred outcome was: they would offer the safety of her family for her co-operation and then, when they had satisfied themselves that she had not kept any of the evidence that she had retrieved from the car, they would execute all three of them. They would leave no clue that might explain what had happened. The police would investigate, find nothing, describe it as a senseless tragedy and close the book.

'What do I have to do to prove it?'

'Let's start with the photographs. Did you copy them?'

'No,' she said.

'And the flash drives? Look at them?'

'No.'

'Copy them?'

'No. I told him I didn't.'

'I know you did. He doesn't believe you.'

Beatrix worked hard to keep her focus clear, but it was almost impossible. Isabella was looking at her with a dumb mixture of incomprehension and terror, and Lucas, while he was fearful and confused too, also wore a look of betrayal and that, Beatrix had to accept, was fair enough. She had always done everything that she could to leave her work at the door; usually, it was possible to leave it at the airport arrivals gate. She had never entertained the possibility that it might find her here.

'You mind if the others have a look around the house?'

'Knock yourselves out.'

'Go upstairs,' Five said to Eight.

He disappeared into the hallway and started upstairs. Beatrix heard Nine and Eleven follow him.

Five looked over at Ten. 'Check the kitchen.'

Beatrix fixed them all in her mind, working out the order she was going to have to attack them: Five, Ten, then whoever came down the stairs first.

'Keep nice and still,' Five said.

She kept the gun aimed at Lucas.

Chapter 8

Beatrix would wonder about what she did next for years afterwards, running the sequence of events through her mind in the squalid rooms and opium dens that would become her home. She knew that this would be the only chance that she had; the odds were against her, and unless she was prepared to sacrifice either her husband or her daughter, she knew, beyond question, that they would all be dead within a matter of minutes. She would wonder, too, during the long lonely nights of her exile when she numbly chased the dragon, whether Lucas had looked at her with a flash of understanding – and perhaps even silent approval – just before she dropped the letter opener down into her hand, spun it and leapt for Five.

Chisholm was trained to act on instinct and the shot, from this range, couldn't possibly miss. The 9mm round struck Lucas in the face, boring a hole in his forehead just above his nose and almost perfectly between his eyes. It was a small mercy that he died immediately and he did not see his wife lunging across the room with the blade clasped in her fist.

Five swung her gun arm around in a blur of motion, preternaturally fast, and fired another shot. The range was too close to miss, again, although Beatrix had anticipated it and arced away from the bullet's track at the final moment; it missed the centre of her body and sliced through the flesh and bone in her left shoulder instead. Her nerves screamed, but the rush of adrenaline drowned them out. She tackled Five, the sudden impact of the collision tipping the armchair over and onto its back, spilling both women onto the floor. Five tried to block Beatrix's downward stab, but her arm was pinned and Beatrix had all the momentum. Their wrists clashed, but Beatrix forced the blade down and down until she couldn't press it down any more.

Isabella screamed, leapt to her feet and ran for the door.

Five's Sig was on the floor; Beatrix reached for it and rolled over onto her back, aiming and firing twice as Ten came back into the room. Her broken ribs impeded her aim and the first shot went wide, splintering the door jamb, but the second hit him in the leg. He dropped his gun and collapsed, falling sideways to the floor.

Five struggled to her haunches and then fell backwards onto her backside. Her head hung forwards, but at an angle, and her breathing came in ragged hisses in and out. Beatrix aimed the gun as Chisholm raised her head and looked at her.

The letter knife was buried halfway into her throat.

There was the sound of hurried movement from upstairs. Beatrix had no time. She got to her feet. Isabella was at the door. Her face and the white dress she was wearing had been sprayed with blowback from the shot that had killed her father.

'Isabella,' Beatrix moaned through the sudden curtain of pain that fell across her. 'Come here, darling.'

She was covered in blood: her own, and Five's.

The girl hesitated.

'Isabella, come to Mummy.'

She took a half-step, but it was too late. The door opened and Eight was there, encircling Isabella's waist with his left arm and aiming the gun at Beatrix's head with the other.

'Drop it!' he said.

Beatrix aimed back at him. 'If you hurt her . . .' she began, the words trailing away.

Nine and Eleven were clattering down the stairs. They would go around through the kitchen and flank her. This was a stand-off she couldn't win.

'Put the gun down,' Eight ordered.

Beatrix ignored him as she backed away. 'Listen to me, very carefully. If anything happens to her – and I mean if you hurt a *single hair on her head* – I'll hunt you down and kill you and everyone you've ever loved. Your wife. Your husband. Your kids. That goes for the rest of you and Control, too. It goes *double* for him. Tell him. The only thing that is going to keep me from doing that is my daughter. If anything happens to her, I'll have nothing to lose.'

Eight nodded. He was wise enough to know when to compromise. 'Fair enough.'

Beatrix held the gun steady, aware that by aiming at Eight she was aiming at her daughter, too.

'Isabella,' she said. 'I want you to listen to me. I want you to go with this man. He's going to look after you. Mummy has to go away now. I don't know for how long, maybe for a long time. But I'll always be watching you. And I will always love you. Very, very much. Do you understand that, baby?'

The girl was only three years old. How could she understand? She had been sitting next to her father as he was shot in the head and then she had watched as her mother had been shot, then stabbed a woman in the throat and shot a man in the leg. If she could understand what she was telling her now, she did not show it; she stared at her dumbly, her mouth slack. Beatrix desperately wanted to remember her blue eyes with their usual sparkle of mischief, but now they were empty and dull.

She backed away, her eyes beginning to blur from the tears, and opened the door to the garden. Ten was on the floor, clutching his leg, and Eight did not come after her; perhaps he was tending to Five, perhaps he recognised that it made more sense to accept the truce. The pain of her wounded shoulder blazed as Beatrix ran into the garden, scattering the chickens pecking at their seed, and clambered up and over the fence and into the garden of the adjacent house beyond.

She thought of Isabella, and the fear and confusion in her priceless face, and choked down a sob as she opened the gate and passed into the road beyond.

PART 2
TEXAS – PRESENT DAY

9

The detective removed the handcuffs from John Milton's wrists and he rubbed the skin where it had chafed against the metal bracelets. The officer dropped the cuffs on the scuffed and scarred surface of the table, went around to the other side, drew back the chair and sat down.

'Sit,' he instructed.

Milton did as he was told.

The detective was young. He couldn't have been that long out of the Academy. Young and fresh and keen to make a name for himself. Just his luck.

There was an old-fashioned tape recorder on the table. The detective tore the plastic sheath from a micro-cassette, took it out of its box and slipped it into the slot. He set the unit to record.

He cleared his throat. 'All right, then. For the record, the speaker is Detective Dennis Bennington of the Victoria Police Department, and, also present, Detective Robert Kenney. The man being interviewed here this afternoon is Mr John Smith. That's S-M-I-T-H. Can I have your address, please, sir?'

'I don't have one.'

'No fixed abode?'

'I'm travelling.'

'I see. And your accent?'

'English.'

'All right, then. Before we get started, you must understand your rights. You have the right to remain silent. Anything you say can be used against you in a court of law. You have the right to talk to a lawyer for advice before we ask you any questions and to have him or her with you during questioning. Do you understand that?'

'I do.'

'If you cannot afford a lawyer, a lawyer will be provided for you at no cost. Do you understand that?'

'Yes.'

Bennington nodded. 'Fair enough. Put your initials right here, please.' He gave Milton a pen and a printed form that noted that he was waiving his rights.

Milton initialled it. 'Can we get on with this, please?'

'You say you're English, but you have an American passport?'

'My mother,' he said. It was a lie. The passport was a fake, but it had been useful to have one as he passed through South America.

'Where were you before you came here?'

'Just got out of San Francisco.'

'How long were you there?'

'Six months, give or take.'

'Doing what?'

'I had a couple of jobs. I worked for an ice distribution company in the day and drove taxis at night.'

'Why did you leave?'

'Is it relevant?'

'Answer the question, please, sir.'

'It was just time to go.'

'And where are you headed?'

'Nowhere in particular. Wherever I end up.'

'All right, then. What did you do before that?'

Milton hesitated. What would they say if he told them the truth? I was an assassin for the British government for the better part of a decade, I killed one hundred and thirty-six men and women, my employer ordered that I be eliminated after I tried to resign and now I'm on the run.

What would two good ole boys make of that? They would think he was insane.

'This and that,' he said instead.

'So why'd you stop in Victoria?'

'I've never been to Texas before,' he replied. 'And it was on my way.'

'So you want to explain what happened in Bill's?'

'You were there, officer. You saw what happened.'

'Why don't you tell me your side of things.' He tapped a finger against the tape machine, spooling quietly on the side of the table. 'For the record.'

Milton sighed with frustration. 'I went to the bar for something to eat and to watch the game on ESPN. It's a nice bar, reasonably busy. I was sitting at the counter, right next to you. You tried to start a conversation about the chicken wings I was eating. The sauce, I think. You said it was good. I agreed, but I wasn't interested in talking to you and, eventually, you got the picture and shut up. I concentrated on the game and my food again. Then two men came into the bar. Big guys. Both drunk and looking for trouble. They went over to a table where three girls were sitting down having a drink and made a nuisance of themselves. Made inappropriate advances. The girls asked them to leave and they didn't. I went over and asked them to stop. I was polite, but I don't think they took too kindly to it. One of them tried to stab me with a broken glass. I banged his face against the table. The other man swung a pool cue at me. I broke his nose. You arrested me. How does that sound, officer? About right?'

'Have you ever met either of the men you attacked before?'

'Never. Have you?'

Bennington shuffled a little in his chair.

'You arrested them, too?' Milton asked.

Bennington shuffled a little uncomfortably. 'No.'

'Who are they?'

'Cliff Manziel and Johnny Robinson.'

Milton frowned. He remembered a sign on the wall as they were booking him last night. 'Manziel – that's the Sheriff's name, isn't it?'

The detective nodded.

'And let me guess – Cliff is his son?'

Milton closed his eyes and smiled. Just his dumb luck: out of all the drunken bullies he could've gotten into a brawl with, he had to pick them. He had no idea the guy was the son of a cop. It probably wouldn't have made a difference, but he might have handled it differently. It would have been funny if it wasn't so inconvenient.

'Did you have any other questions?' he asked the detectives.

'Not now.'

'So what's next?'

'We arrange a bail hearing for you.'

'And until then?'

'You'll be transferred to the county lockup. It'll be a couple of days before we can get you in front of a judge.'

Milton sighed. He'd beaten the son of the local sheriff. That couldn't possibly be good. If daddy was upset, and he *would* be upset, he was going to want to get some revenge. That spelt trouble. He could imagine what it might mean for him in the short term: a few good ole boys in an empty cell back at the lockup, a fight where he would be badly outnumbered and retaliating would just make things worse for him. He would have to suck it up and take it. And what then, assuming they didn't put him in the hospital? The judge would undoubtedly be a friend of the sheriff. The jury, if it was to be a jury trial, would look at him as an outsider who thought it was acceptable to start bar brawls with the sons of local dignitaries. Texas was an insular kind of place. That kind of thing was probably a big deal. All kinds of witnesses would turn up to say that the attack was unprovoked. He would end up convicted and in the penitentiary, just like that, looking at a long stint in some dismal establishment.

Although, of course, it would never get to that.

Milton doubted whether he would even get to the bail hearing. Control would find him before two days were up. His prints and personal details had been taken when they booked him last night. They would have been transferred by now, passed between servers, an electronic handshake that would trigger an alarm somewhere. The Group had located him easily enough when he was in Ciudad Juárez and that had been a pit. How much simpler would it be to find him in Texas?

Options? Milton looked around the room. It was secure – bars across the window, a double-locked door – no obvious way for him to get out. Bennington and Kenney were armed, but he would have been able to disable them both without much difficulty, but where would that get him? What would he do then? He was inside a locked room in a police station. Even if he managed to escape, how far would he be able to get? Victoria was a town he didn't know. He had no means of transport. He had looked out of the window as they brought him to the interview room. It was mid-morning and the sun was already burning bright, heatwaves radiating off the scorched ground. Not the kind of weather to be hiking across open country. He figured he'd have five minutes to find a ride before the locals had enough time to raise a posse and come after him. Five minutes, maybe ten if he was lucky.

And then what?

It was pointless. Hopeless. He was going to have to let things play out. He started to prepare himself for the inevitable: a beating and then, much worse, whatever would happen to him when the Group finally found him. Forced rendition back to London if he was lucky; a bribed guard to press a shiv into his heart in the penitentiary showers if he wasn't.

It turned out he was wrong about that; he was wrong about all of it. It turned out that he was wrong about a lot of things, and his day was about to take an unexpected turn.

10

It was early evening when Milton heard footsteps approaching down the corridor. He had been lying on the squalid cot, staring up at the ceiling. The bugs had come out of the cracks and were marching across the ceiling two by two. He lay there, his fingers laced beneath his head, watching them with vague disinterest, when he heard the cage door at the end of the corridor open and close. He swung his legs off the bed and stood, bracing himself. *Here they come.*

The key turned in the lock and the door swung open.

It was Bennington. He was alone.

'What is it?'

'Up you get, partner.'

'What for?'

'You're free to go. The charges have been dropped. Come with me, please.'

Milton hid his surprise. He followed Bennington out of the cell, along the corridor and out into the office beyond. There was a desk, two chairs and a couch pushed up against the wall. A woman was sitting on the couch. Medium height, slender build, long legs, lots of red hair. Milton had never seen her before.

Bennington touched his hand to a cardboard box on the desk. 'Here are your things,' he said.

Milton looked inside: his wallet, cigarette lighter, leather jacket and shoelaces.

'Sign for them, please.'

Milton signed the form and took his belongings.

The woman stood. 'Mr Smith?'

'Yes?'

'My name is Frances Delaney. I'm with the Federal Bureau of Investigation.'

'How can I help you?'

She paused and turned to Bennington. 'Is that all, detective?'

'Yes, ma'am. He's free to go.'

'Thank you. Mr Smith, will you come with me, please?

Milton was confused; he had anticipated several possible outcomes and this was certainly not one of them.

Delaney stepped across the office, through the public waiting room beyond and then into the hot night outside.

Milton looked around: he had been driven to the station in the back of a patrol car and it had been daylight. It looked different at night. Neon displays glowed above the entrance to bars and clubs. Youngsters hung out of car windows as they cruised down Main Street. A Lexus with blacked out windows was parked against the curb.

'What's going on?' he asked her.

'Get in the car, Captain Milton.'

'I'm sorry?'

'Let's dispense with that, shall we? I'm sure you'd rather get away from here?'

'How do you know my name?'

'I'm not from the FBI, Captain Milton. You're fortunate that you were arrested in a place like this. Somewhere they'd leave an officer like *that* to look after you. I've managed to pull the wool over his eyes, but it won't stand up to scrutiny for too long. It'd be better if we got moving.'

'How did you find me?'

'I'll tell you later. I'll tell you everything you want to know.'

'No,' he said. 'I'm not going anywhere until you tell me what you want.'

'Just to talk, Captain Milton. Get in the car, please.'

She took the key fob from her bag and blipped the door. She crossed the pavement and opened the driver's side door.

Milton paused, working out the angles. He looked out at Main Street, the cars rolling slowly by in either direction. There was a bar nearby, the sound of loud music and raucous, unfriendly hollering spilling out. It was a boiling-hot evening: fighting weather. The place suddenly felt charged and hostile. The sheriff was still around, plus his boy. He didn't know what Delaney had pulled to get him out, but he didn't doubt that if he stayed and ran across the Manziels there would be nothing to prevent them from settling the scores. If they found out that he had been freed by deception, they would come after him. It would be even worse.

He would have to leave. He would walk back to his hotel, collect his things and catch the first Greyhound out of town. Or he could go straight to Hertz, hire a car and drive himself away. He would do that. Delaney was intriguing, but he hadn't lasted as long as he had by trusting good-looking women he had never met before.

'Thanks for your help. I'll take my chances.'

She shook her head. 'I know about the Group, Captain Milton. I know how close they were to catching up with you in Mexico.'

He fought to maintain a nonchalant front. 'I don't know what you mean.'

'There are some things you need to know. You should know that they're already in the country. There are four of them. They flew out of RAF Northolt last night and landed in Houston an hour ago. They're driving here now. The last I heard, they were in Ganado. That's not far. They'll be here in thirty minutes. How far do you think you'll get with them on your tail?'

Milton tried hard to hide his discomfort.

'Captain Milton – John. Get in the car, please. I'd rather not be here when they arrive. And I'll tell you everything you want to know.'

There was something about Delaney that made him want to hear her out.

'All right,' he said.

He stepped into the street and got into the other side of the Lexus.

11

They drove for half an hour. If Delaney wanted conversation, then she was happy to wait to get it started. She paused behind a truck until the road ahead was clear and then pulled out behind it without a word.

Milton took a moment to check out the interior of the Lexus. It was a four-door, a big executive number, very fancy. He would have guessed it was six months' old; it still had the smell of a new car and it was kept in good shape. The leather had that deep smell that spoke eloquently of money and the glass was tinted black like a hearse. There were two small suitcases on the back seat. They were identical Samsonite models, the kind of wheeled design favoured by business travellers who prefer to avoid checking their things into the hold. A garment cover was hooked on the handle above the right-hand rear door.

The road became a three-lane interstate and Delaney accelerated up to seventy.

'Comfortable?' she asked him.

'Fine. How long are we going to be driving for?'

'About an hour.'

The seat was motorised. Milton pressed the rocker button on the door and, with a hum of its motor, the seat slid back a few inches. Might as well stretch his legs out; he didn't know what he was going to find when they got to where they were going and the last thing he wanted was to have his muscles cramp up.

He thought about what Delaney had said. He had no idea how she could have known about the Group, but, if what she said was true, she had probably saved his life.

He gazed out through the window at the sparse traffic heading into Victoria as they sped away from it. The lights of the cars and trucks shone brightly, high beams raking into the sky until the drivers approached and flicked them down. He looked at them and wondered if he would see a face that he recognised.

Delaney glanced into the rear-view mirror at the traffic behind them and changed lanes. Milton took the chance to look at her reflection in the windscreen. She was average height, slim and had a delicately boned face. The auburn hair was the most striking thing about her: long and glossy, all the way down past her shoulders. He guessed she was a hundred and thirty pounds and five-nine. Age? Somewhere between thirty or thirty-five, he thought, although he'd never been good at guessing women's ages. Her eyes were vivid emerald, her skin was flawless with little make-up. She was very striking. She was wearing a trouser suit with a white shirt that had a prominent collar. It was simple and elegant and obviously expensive. Her hands were slender and her nails were polished and manicured. She didn't wear a wedding ring. The only jewellery she wore was a discreet silver cross around her neck.

'Where are we going?' he asked her.

'Houston,' she said.

12

Delaney had booked two rooms at a motor court that served the airport. They arrived at eleven; she checked in while Milton waited in the car. He wondered whether he should disappear now, open the door and fade into the busy night, but he resisted the temptation. She knew too much about him and about things she should never have known for him not to be just a little intrigued. Instead, he arched his back and reached into the rear of the car for the nearest suitcase. He unzipped it quickly and pulled open the lid. There was nothing there, save for a couple of changes of clothes, two pairs of shoes and a toilet bag.

He settled back into the front and opened the glove compartment: he took out the car's manual and insurance details and put them to the side. There was some documentation from a rental agency; the car had been hired yesterday from the Hertz counter at the airport. The documents were signed in her name. Whoever Delaney was, she had flown in to pick him up. There was nothing else in the compartment, and so Milton put the documents back and shut it.

Delaney returned. She put the car into gear and rolled into the parking lot next to a low single-storey terrace that was divided into a dozen rooms. She reverse-parked the car into a space and switched off the engine.

'We've got that one and that one,' she said, pointing towards two adjacent rooms. 'Are you hungry?'

He was; he hadn't eaten all day. 'I could eat.'

'You could probably do with a shower, too. Why don't you go in and get yourself sorted. I'll order some delivery and then we can talk.'

'All right,' he said.

They both exited the car.

Delaney opened the rear door and removed the suitcases and the garment holder. She draped the holder over the extended handle of one of the cases. 'That's for you,' she said. 'There's a change of clothes in the suitcase and some toiletries. There's a suit in the holder. You'll need to wear it tomorrow.'

'What am I doing tomorrow?'

'Get freshened up. I'll explain later.'

13

The room was exactly what Milton would have expected to find in a low-budget motel. There was a bed; a desk with a chair; a television on the desk; a kettle with little sachets of tea and coffee and sweeteners.

Milton hauled the suitcase onto the bed and opened it: three pairs of boxer shorts and three white T-shirts, still wrapped in paper; three pairs of thick woollen socks; a pair of leather brogues; a pair of Timberlands; two pairs of Levis; a pair of fur-lined gloves; a thick woollen scarf; a new toiletries bag with a comb, a toothbrush, a full tube of toothpaste, a pack of disposable razors and a bottle of shaving cream. It looked as if Delaney had stopped at the shop on her way through the airport and, knowing that he was incarcerated and likely had nothing with him, had bought everything that she thought that he might need.

He unzipped the garment carrier and took out the items that were inside. There was a charcoal Hugo Boss suit, single-breasted, expensive, and a thick overcoat. He checked the tags: the measurements were more or less what he would have ordered if he was buying it for himself.

What *didn't* she know about him?

He looked at the socks, the gloves, the scarf and the coat. They weren't chosen for Texas weather.

Where did she want him to go?

Milton undressed and went into the bathroom. It was simple and clean and he stood beneath the shower for twenty minutes, letting the hot water slew off the sweat and grime that had accumulated over the course of the last couple of days. He scrubbed his face, softening the stubble that abraded his palms, and then spread on a handful of the cream and shaved.

He turned off the tap, wrapped a towel around his waist and stood at the mirror. His eyes were a cold greyish blue, his mouth had a twist to it that could sometimes make him look cruel and there was a long horizontal scar from his cheek to the start of his nose, the memento of a knife fight in a Honolulu bar. There were other scars all across his body. His hair was long and a little unkempt. The job hauling ice around San Francisco had improved his fitness and there was more definition in his arms and shoulders now than there had been since he had stopped working for the Group.

He turned away from the mirror, catching a quick glimpse of the angel's wings tattooed across his back, and changed into a fresh T-shirt and a pair of jeans from the suitcase. They fit him well. Delaney knew exactly what she was doing.

He pulled the door closed behind him and crossed the veranda to the room next door. He knocked, twice, and heard the soft footfalls as Delaney approached. She took the door off the chain, opened it and welcomed him inside.

Milton scanned the room. Force of habit. It was an analogue of his own, just in reverse; the furniture was arranged on the right, not the left. He went over to the bathroom and checked inside. It was the same as his, and empty.

'Relax,' she told him. 'It's just you and me.'

'You'll have to excuse me,' he said. 'I've no idea who you are. Being here is against my better judgement.'

'So why are you here?'

'Let's just say you've got my attention.'

'I've ordered burgers. I hope that's all right?'

'Fine.'

'You want to sit?'

'No,' he replied. 'I'll stand.'

'Okay,' she said. 'But I'm going to sit. We've got a lot to talk about.'

She sat down on the edge of the bed. Milton leant back against the wall.

'Who are you?' he asked. 'Really?'

'My name is Anna Vasil'yevna Kushchyenko. I work for the SVR.'

'You're Russian intelligence.'

'That's right, Captain Milton.'

'Which Directorate?'

'Is that really important?'

'It is if you don't want me to walk out of that door and disappear.'

'Directorate S.'

'Operations?'

'Correct.'

Milton couldn't help the smile.

'What is it?'

'This is the first time I've been busted out of jail by a Russian spook. What are you – a sleeper?'

'For the last ten years.'

'Frances Delaney.'

She smiled. 'That's me.'

'But not FBI?'

'No. That was just a useful story.'

'Okay, Anna. You better tell me why you risked your cover to get me out of there. You know I'm not going to talk to you.'

'It would be easier if I showed you,' she said.

She got up, crossed the room to her suitcase and removed an iPad. She activated it and jabbed her finger against the screen until she had opened the attachment to an email. She handed the tablet to Milton, the screen realigning as he held it up to look at it. It was a photograph of a man. He had short cropped black hair shot through with threads of silver and grey, a slab-like forehead and a nose that had been broken too many times. He had been beaten: his right eye was closed up, a livid purple bruise around the socket. There was a bloody welt on the side of his forehead and abrasions scraped down his left cheek. He was staring into the camera, the defiance on his face belying the punishment that had been meted out to him.

'Do you know him?' Anna asked.

Milton gritted his teeth and tightened his grip on the tablet. 'Yes,' he said.

The man in the picture was Captain Michael Pope.

Anna watched Milton's reaction. 'We know you and Captain Pope have history. You were in the army at the same time. You are the same age, give or take a year or two, and you were both in Iraq during the first war, although you were in different battalions. Once the war was over, Captain Pope transferred into the First Battalion, B Company. The same Company, the same rifle platoon as you. You served in Northern Ireland together.'

Milton dropped the tablet back on the bed. 'Very good,' he said. 'You've done your research.'

'We know that he joined Group Fifteen a little while after you. An excellent reputation, although not in the same league as you, Captain Milton, of course. We believe he replaced you as Number One after you left. Is that correct?'

'You can't expect me to comment on that.'

'No, I suppose not. And nor do I need you to. We know.'

'So stop wasting my time. Are you going to tell me what happened to him?'

'Captain Pope was arrested two months ago in Monaco. He entered the country with a false passport. He was apprehended with a Barrett M1 sniper rifle and a hundred rounds of ammunition. The weapon with which you made your name, I understand? The operation in North Korea?'

'Again . . .' Milton said, shrugging.

Anna ignored his reticence. 'He was transferred to Moscow. He has been questioned, of course. At great length. He has been as' – she searched for the right word – 'stoical as you would expect a man of his training to be, in the circumstances.

We believe that his purpose in France was to assassinate my commanding officer. He has a holiday home there. Captain Pope had hired a motorboat. We believe his plan was to take the boat adjacent to his estate and make the shot from there. An audacious attempt, had it been allowed to proceed. Our experts considered it foolish, apart from those familiar with the skill of your country's cleaners. It would take tremendous skill to snipe a target from a moving boat. You, perhaps, Captain Milton . . . a shot that you would have taken?'

Milton said nothing. He looked down at the bed, at the tablet, at Pope's battered and bloodied face. The last time he had seen him was in Juárez. Pope had orders to bring him back to London, dead or alive. It would have been easier to have shot him – the agent they sent after him, Callan, had wanted to – but Pope had forbidden it. There was no question about it: they were on different sides now, but he had saved Milton's life.

'Where is he?'

'In a Siberian gulag. You will be aware of the quality of life an inmate in a gulag can expect. If he survives five years, I would be surprised.'

Milton nodded. He knew he was being baited. 'You know so much about us, you must know that we're not on the best of terms. He still works for the government. I don't. We have nothing in common.'

'Please, Captain, I don't believe that. You have a long shared history. I can't believe that stands for nothing. And there is an alternative for him. Freedom is not impossible, even for a man for whom there is no question of his guilt.'

Again, Milton said nothing.

'Are you not interested?'

'I don't like being played, Anna, and you would be wasting your time.'

'We know what happened between you and Control. We know that you tried to leave the Group and that he wants you dead because of it. All we want is the chance to talk to you. We have some questions which require answers. We would not ask for any operational knowledge and no agent will be put at risk. You might consider yourself to be a consultant. Some of the questions, if you answer them, they will embarrass Control, but mightn't that be of use to you? We know that his stock is not high with your government at the moment. Your absconding has damaged his reputation. If he was replaced, perhaps the standing order to have you killed would be rescinded, too?'

'I doubt that.'

'Nevertheless . . .'

'What questions?'

'That is not for me to say. My superior wants to speak to you. His name is Colonel Shcherbatov. Do you know him?'

'No.'

'He is in Moscow. It would not be a simple thing for him to come here. Not as simple as it would be for me, in any event.'

'You want me to go to Moscow?'

'There is a flight from Houston to New York in the morning. We would take it and then transit to a flight to Moscow. I have a new passport for you. A cover story, should one be needed.'

'I'm not going to Moscow,' Milton said. 'You're out of your mind.'

'Think about Captain Pope. Think about what you could do for him. He has a wife, I understand. Two young children. You have it in your power to return their father to them. Sleep on it, Captain Milton. See if you feel the same way in the morning. Perhaps you will have changed your mind.'

PART 3
RUSSIA

14

The jumbo circled over Sheremetyevo, slowly negotiating its way down the stack of jetliners, and then the fuselage shook a little as the undercarriage was lowered. Milton stowed his tray table and slid the copy of *The Hound of the Baskervilles* that he had purchased from the airport bookshop into his bag. Anna was sitting three rows ahead of him; he could see the top of her head, the crown of red hair easily visible in the dimmed cabin lights.

He looked out of the window at the huge, sprawling expanse of Moscow. The lights of the city stretched away into the far distance: a seemingly interminable grid of streets, darkened holes marking the public parks, the serpentine slither of the Moskva, white smoke spewing from the smokestacks of the power plant on its bank. The rows of Stalin's wedding-cake skyscrapers were covered over with the snow that was piling down from the thick, angry clouds through which they had just descended. Milton saw the onion domes of the Kremlin, topped with their lurid red stars; the basilica of St Basil's on Red Square, a child's toy at this altitude. Everything was mantled in white.

They landed and proceeded through border control with suspicious ease. They already had their luggage and so Milton followed Anna as she led the way through the glitzy terminal building, replete with Russia's new wealth, and outside to the taxi rank. The bitter air swept around him again. Milton had spent a winter in Moscow, five years ago, during an assignment that took four months from preparation to bloody completion, and he knew what a Russian winter meant. He thought of Pope and what Anna had told him; if he really had been stuffed into a Siberian gulag, this weather – which would still be brutal – would be a balmy sojourn in comparison to what *he* could expect.

The taxi driver had a tiny five-inch television fixed to the dashboard, sucking power from the cigarette lighter. There was a football match taking place – CSKA were playing Munich in the Champions League – and he carried on watching it, occasionally raising his eyes to check the traffic ahead of him.

Anna sat next to Milton, staring out of the window as the streets rolled by them. She had freshened up in the toilet at the airport, applying a fresh coat of lipstick and refreshing her scent. Her right leg was crossed over her left, the expensively shod foot dangled inches from Milton's calf. The fingers of her left hand, the nails blood red, were spread out on her knee.

Milton wondered whether she had been instructed to sleep with him.

The driver turned off Tverskaya Street and pulled up outside the Ritz-Carlton. The pavements had been scrupulously swept clear of the snow that was so thick elsewhere and the uniformed porters hurried to help them as they stepped outside. Milton politely brushed them off as Anna paid the fare.

'We will stay here tonight,' she said as they followed their luggage inside.

'When do we see the colonel?'

'Tomorrow morning.'

'Fine. I'll see you in the morning.'

'There's one other thing. We would prefer it if you would stay in the room.'

'I'm a prisoner?'

'No, of course not.'

'But . . .'

'But we would prefer it if you did not go out tonight. The meeting tomorrow is important, for your friend, especially. You should be well rested. Perhaps you could order room service and get an early night?'

'Yes,' Milton said. 'I am tired. Perhaps I will.'

15

Milton stood, pulled aside the net curtains and stared out into the cold night beyond. His room was on the fifteenth floor, but the panorama was constrained by the blizzard of snowflakes that were being whipped around the building by the harsh wind. The view would open a little as the wind paused: long streets with street lamps casting bowls of golden light against the white; the glowing tail lights of cars and trucks and buses; tall buildings with some windows lit, others switched off by orders of the municipal government in an attempt to avoid the brown-outs that still afflicted the city.

Milton gazed out over the streets for five minutes, allowing his memory to drift. He was much too young to have been involved in the Cold War, but there had been plenty of missions inside the borders of the new Russia and the satellite states that still clung to it like piglets suckling the teats of their mother. He remembered a particular assignment in Moscow a year or two after he had been transferred into the Group. He and Number Four had entered the country under the cover of diplomatic passports and had taken rooms at the Hilton Leningradskaya, not too far from the hotel where he was staying now. An arms fair was taking place, and their target – a dealer who was negotiating the terms of a deal that would secure advanced surface-to-air missiles for the Iranian regime – was going to be in attendance. Number Four had driven the motorcycle, with Milton riding pillion. He had emptied the magazine of his H&K into the dealer's BMW, killing him but sparing his mistress and his driver.

Milton turned from the window and sat on the edge of the bed. He thought of Anna Vasil'yevna Kushchyenko in the room next to his. What would she be doing? Making her report to her superior officers, informing them that she had successfully delivered him into the country? Her room would be identical to his and he thought of her on the bed, most likely adjacent to his and separated by the wall. Six inches away, perhaps. She was very attractive. He would have been lying to himself if he said that he did not find her beguiling. That, no doubt, was why they had sent her. He thought of le Carré's books or the films about espionage from the sixties and seventies; she was the lissom girl sent to guarantee his attendance, the honeytrap in the Cold War thriller. He wondered what would happen if he stepped into the corridor and knocked on her door. He did not doubt that she would welcome him inside. It was tempting and there would be no harm in it, an interesting diversion to kill the time until tomorrow, but Milton resisted.

There were things he had to do. An old friend to meet, and information to gather.

* * *

Milton dressed in the warm clothes that Anna had provided, pulled on the Timberland boots and put on his thick overcoat, quietly shut his door and padded softly to the lift. He took it down to the ground floor and, without pausing, strode across the lobby, down the small flight of stairs, through the revolving door and into the street outside. He had noticed the man sitting in an armchair next to an open fire, a copy of the *Herald-Tribune* spread out in front of him. He had chosen a spot where he could observe the door and the lobby and Milton pegged him as an agent from the internal security directorate immediately. Milton hadn't rushed through the lobby – he didn't want them to think he was trying to flee, a reason to call for backup – but neither had he dawdled. As he emerged onto the street outside, he made a show of arranging his overcoat, fastening the buttons all the way to the top and, as he looped his scarf around his neck and tucked it into the front of the coat, he allowed himself a quarter-turn back to the interior and saw the man, without his newspaper, coming down the steps.

The snow was falling thick and heavy, fat flakes that settled on everything, softening edges, turning the parked cars into sculptures with gracefully curved lines. It was deep; a trough had been shovelled down the centre of the pavements that was wide enough for two people to pass, the walls of snow and ice on either side reaching up to Milton's knees. He walked at a decent pace, following streets that he remembered from the last time he had been here.

He stopped at a currency exchange and swapped two of the hundred-dollar bills in his pocket for roubles. He turned to the street as the cashier counted out his money and saw the man from the hotel a hundred feet behind him, talking into the open window of a Mercedes SUV that was parked against the bank of snow on the roadside edge of the pavement. Reinforcements, Milton thought. Fair enough. It didn't concern him.

He took the notes from the cashier, put them into his pocket and set off again for the station at Ploshchad Revolyutsii. He stepped into the relative warmth inside the heavy glass doors and bought a fur-trimmed *ushanka* from the stallholder who was doing a brisk trade flogging hats, scarves and gloves to credulous tourists. Milton put the hat in his pocket, bought a day ticket for the trains and made his way to the platform.

A second tail got ahead of him, probably alerted by a call from the agent in the car. He was waiting on the platform. Milton recognised him as an intelligence man without very much difficulty. He was standing alone at the end of the platform where the statues were; the proud revolutionaries with their puffed-out chests and bulging biceps. It was the obvious spot for him to wait; he would have a good view of new arrivals. He was glancing at a newspaper that he obviously wasn't reading, speaking the odd word from the side of his mouth into a throat mike hidden beneath the scarf around his neck. The Russians used to have plenty of good men. Times had changed; now that the prestige and influence of the security service had been affected by the fall of the Wall, they had plenty of bad ones too, and more of the latter than the former. They were bad ones tonight.

Milton thought, a little ruefully, it might have been nice to have been assigned some professionals to keep an eye on him. More of a challenge to lose them and, he admitted to himself, he'd been out of the game for a year; it would have been good for his ego to know that he still demanded their full attention.

Never mind.

Milton walked towards the man and looked into his eyes for a moment before he clocked him and turned away. Milton wasn't concerned that the man knew that his cover had been blown. He wanted him to know. His ego again.

Milton looked across the tracks to the other platform and waited until the display board advertised a wait of a minute for the eastbound train. He remembered the station well from the times he had been active in Moscow and its geography came back to him without difficulty. He turned on his heel and walked quickly to the stairs that transferred passengers to the green line. He took the steps two at a time, quite sure that he would have sent the man on the platform into a spin and enjoying that knowledge.

He turned his head as he reached the middle of the bridge that crossed the tracks: on his left, he could see the collection of chandeliers, running away down the platform and, eventually, into the darkened maw of the tunnel from which the trains emerged; on his right was the corresponding walkway that offered a way to cross the line from the other side of the platform. It was close enough for him to see the agent hurrying up the stairs, walking quickly but not daring to run. He was still being careful, even as he was fearful he was going to lose his target. Perhaps he didn't know that he had been blown; if that was right, that just made him even more pitiable.

The train wheezed into the station, the doors sliding open on runners that could have done with a drop of oil, and Milton embarked. It was just two stops to Pushkinskaya. He looked at the etiolated panelling and the strip lighting that flickered and cut out at regular intervals.

Eastbound and westbound trains at Pushkinskaya pulled into different sides of the same platform and a second train was drawing to a halt just as the doors of Milton's train opened. He walked across the platform, quickly obscured by the emerging throng of passengers, bundled up in their thick parkas and muffled hats. He boarded the westbound train.

Milton took the *ushanka* and pulled it onto his head, untying the ear flaps from the crown and straightening them all the way out, enough to obscure his face. He looked down at his feet, yet glanced at the platform through the corner of his eye as the train jerked and bumped into motion. He saw the agent, confused and lost, caught between the eastbound and westbound trains, unsure which one he needed to be on. Had Milton changed trains or had he stayed where he was?

The train slid away, Milton looking down again to hide his face as the agent passed by his window, and then they were back into the tunnel and accelerating in the direction from which he had arrived.

16

Milton sat in the seat, running his fingers over the rough, threadbare upholstery. He looked up and down the train and, satisfied that he was not being followed, settled back to look at the advertisements that appeared to offer cures for indigestion and hair loss and sexual dysfunction that were neatly arranged beneath the line of the ceiling. He could have been on a train in London, or anywhere else in the world.

His eyes drifted down to the woman sitting opposite him and, for a moment, their eyes held. She was dressed in form-fitting blue jeans, ankle-length fur-trimmed boots and a winter coat with brass buttons that might have looked good from a distance but, up close, looked like it was made out of cheap fabric and probably came from a Chinese or Korean sweatshop. The girl was definitely checking him out. Had she pegged him as a foreigner? Probably. He wasn't dressed to blend in, and the hat looked like something a tourist would wear, not a native Muscovite. It didn't matter. He gave her a careful smile; she smiled back, a little aloof, in that way that Russian girls have, and then he angled his head back to the advertisements and ignored her.

Milton rode the train for a single stop and alighted at Pushkinskaya. He scanned the platform, saw nothing that gave him cause for concern, and navigated the burrow-like tunnels until he found the escalator to the street. There was revolutionary art on the walls of the escalator shaft, striking images of farmhands and soldiers and housewives with powerful forearms that would put wrestlers to shame. It was lit by a row of impressive chandeliers and folk music was playing over the loudspeaker.

He pushed through the heavy glass Metro doors and emerged into the freezing cold of Pushkin Square. He was on Strastnoy Bulvar, the old road that ran around the Kremlin with dark reaches of park between the lanes. A big office block dominated the multi-laned junction, fifteen-foot high letters that spelled out NOKIA anchored to the roof. Neon glared against the snow and the ice.

Milton turned to the south, crossed the gridlocked road and made his way along Tverskoy Boulevard. Four-by-fours crawled up and down the road, white sheets of ice stubbornly resisting the grit, tyres crunching across compacted snow, snow chains rattling, the headlights casting yellow fingers across the dirty white. It was bitterly cold – a digital thermometer in the windows of a pharmacy showed fifteen degrees below zero – and Milton quickly wished he had a more substantial coat. The freezing air settled across the exposed skin of his face, painful within moments. He wouldn't be able to stay out in this weather for long.

He extended his arm to hail a taxi. Three passed by without stopping until a fourth saw him shivering on the pavement and glided into the kerb, the dented mudguard crunching up against the wall of piled snow.

The driver was from Ukraine; there was a flag on the dashboard next to a miniature religious icon. He stank of vodka and there was a bottle wedged into the space between the two front seats. Milton had taken rides with plenty of drunken taxi drivers in Eastern Europe and the fact that he had not been killed – so far – was enough for him to be sanguine about it.

Milton fastened his seat belt quietly, avoiding the implicit criticism of the man's driving that he would have signalled had he made it obvious. He gave the address and settled into the seat as the car picked up speed, the driver ignoring the treacherous conditions as the speedometer ticked up to fifty. They were swallowed by the tunnel that cut beneath the Novy Arbat, and then emerged to speed past the Gogol statue. The driver was honest enough and, rather than taking the circuitous route that many would have chosen, picked a direct route to the Kropotkinskaya Metro station.

Milton gave the driver fifty roubles and another twenty on top and stepped out into the cold. The car had been pleasant in comparison to the arctic blast that greeted him again, quickly chasing away the warmth that he had managed to nurture.

The dark curve of the river was laid out beyond the road. The area had been taken over by floating restaurants over the past decade and Milton had eaten here on many occasions.

Gorky Park was on the other side of the river, although it was invisible tonight, hidden behind the shifting, dense curtain of snow. He half fancied that he could see the neon-tinged outline of the Krymsky Bridge. Beyond that, although he couldn't make it out, would be the floodlit statue of Peter the Great that the Russians had thrown up in the middle of the river. Milton might even have felt a twinge of nostalgia for the old place if it wasn't for the cold that had already made a mockery of his hopelessly inadequate coat.

* * *

The Armenian supermarket was two hundred yards from the entrance to the Metro. It was on the ground floor of a four-storey building with apartments arranged on the three floors above it. It was years since Milton had last visited, but it was all just the same: more goods on the shelves than there had been before, perhaps, but everything was just a little down at heel, a little dusty and dowdy, all a little out of date. The aisles were lit by harsh yellow strip-lights that hung from the ceiling on metal chains. The shoppers shuffled between the shelves, the brutal cold knocking the stuffing from them, the melted snow leaving puddles on the linoleum floor.

Milton made his way down the middle of the shop and opened the door to the storeroom at the rear. There were trays of produce stacked on pallets, the cellophane wrappers cut away with knives, spoiled goods thrown into a pile near the loading bay.

The office was at the other end of the storeroom and he knocked twice, waiting for permission to enter.

'Yes,' the voice said in harshly accented Russian.

Milton pushed the door open and stepped into the small room beyond. There was a desk with a computer, two filing cabinets and a slit-like window that opened onto the litter-infested alleyway at the rear of the supermarket. The room was lit by a single naked bulb. An old FM radio stood on one of the cabinets, tuned to a news channel, the voice of the announcer obscured by the regular bursts and burbles of interference. There was a chair before the desk and sitting in it was a woman who looked to be in her late sixties. She was short and stout with a heavily wrinkled face and a bowl of grey hair that was shot through with streaks of silver. She was dressed practically: sensible black shoes with a decent tread, thick stockings and a worn woollen skirt and sweater that had been chosen for comfort rather than style. She had kind, wise, sad eyes.

'John?'

'*Mamotchka,*' he said, smiling. It meant 'mother' in Russian. Her given name was Anya Dostovalov, but mother was what he had called the old woman for years.

'My God,' she said, pushing herself out of the chair and crossing the room to enfold him in an embrace.

She smelled the same as he remembered: the floral perfume was a trigger that always threw him back to the times he had spent in the East.

She put her arms on his shoulders and held him back a little so that she could get a better look at his face. He smiled into her eyes and dipped his head so that she could kiss him on both cheeks. 'My God,' she repeated, shaking her head. 'I did not think I ever see you again.'

'*Mamotchka,*' he chided, unable to prevent the smile that twitched the sides of his mouth. 'You didn't think I'd forget about you, did you?'

'I hear what happen. What happen in London.'

'You probably heard their version of it.'

'You must tell me. I hear stories, many stories, you are right, but you must tell what really happened. We will have cup of tea, yes?'

'Something warm would be good.'

'And have you eaten, Vanya?'

John was translated as Ivan in Russian, and Vanya was the affectionate diminutive that replaced Ivan. She had used that for him for all the time that they had known each other.

'I haven't.'

'Then we must go upstairs. To apartment. I cook for you.'

17

Anya spoke to the two members of staff on the checkout desk, telling them that they would be locking up tonight without her, opened a door and led Milton up a narrow flight of stairs to the first floor. The doors to a half-dozen apartments faced onto a sparse and ascetic lobby; snow was melting on the boots that had been left on mats outside. Anya took the key that she wore on a thin chain around her neck and unlocked her door. Milton remembered the apartment beyond: parquet floor, a faded and moth-eaten rug and a small chandelier. *Mamotchka* took off her shoes and Milton did the same, following her further into the apartment.

There was a bedroom with a single bed, plus a pine wardrobe and dressing-table set that was scattered with cosmetics and scents. The tiny bathroom was next and then, at the end of the corridor, a sitting room with a small kitchen arranged at one end. The kitchen was equipped with an old-fashioned stove, a tiny fridge and a stovetop kettle. The sitting room had yet more of the parquet floor, softened by another rug. There was a mushroom-shaped water stain that had spread across the ceiling, peeling the plaster away, and a bookshelf with communist-era travelogues and histories. The windows looked down onto the snow-choked streets below.

'Now, John,' she said, gesturing towards the sofa. 'Sit. I prepare food and tea.'

Milton sat and watched as she went about her business. He had known Anya Dostovalov for almost a decade and she had been an asset of British intelligence for far longer than that. Her role had always been as a 'cut-out'. She would stand between a spy and his or her source so that, were her role to be uncovered, she would only be able to identify the sender and the recipient of information. She acted as insulation for the network that MI6 had built, protecting its agents from exposure. The role was critically important and exposed her to considerable risk; once Milton had grown to know and respect her, he was loath to put her in harm's way. Her response had always been to politely yet firmly brush his concerns away. She had been doing this for years, she would say. She knew what she was doing.

She brought over a teapot, a samovar filled with hot water and two cups, and prepared the tea. She had brewed it strong and poured small shots into the cups, topping them up with boiling water from the samovar. Milton sipped his, the taste sharp and bitter and not particularly pleasant to his palate, but the warmth was welcome in his belly.

Anya took her own tea to the kitchen and worked with quick and silent efficiency, emptying out the contents of the tiny fridge and assembling a small buffet for them both: slivers of fish and hunks of pork, pieces of bitter Russian chocolate, a collection of warm blinis, sour cream, the sweet cheese that the Russians liked so much that Milton knew you were supposed to eat with the tea. When she was finished, she brought it over on a wooden tray and set it down on the low coffee table.

'You still remember how to find shop,' she said as she sat down.

'Of course. I'm not likely to forget, am I?'

'You were not followed?'

'Please,' he smiled. 'You know me better than that.'

'I am sorry, Vanya,' she said. 'I have reason to be careful.'

'How do you mean?'

'The ... how do you say? The climate is difficult. Everyone knew KGB was bad, but SVR is just the same.' She smiled. 'And I am too old for gulag.'

'You're not old, *Mamotchka*.'

'Bless you, Vanya, but I am seventy-three. Old woman now.'

'There's no need to worry. I was followed, but I lost them on the Metro. They don't know where I am.'

He sipped the fragrant tea, feeling its warmth in his belly. She waited patiently as he finished the cup and then poured him another.

'So, dear one. What has happened to you?'

He told her. He told her about the assignment in the French Alps and the two Iraqi scientists that he had assassinated and about the little boy who had hidden in the footwell of the car that he had sprayed with bullets, and about the *gendarme* who had been unlucky enough to have been in the wrong place at the wrong time. He told her how he had lost himself in the

93

boy's brown eyes and how he had seen an unbroken line that connected all his victims all the way back to another little boy he had seen in the desert years ago. He told her how he had decided there and then that he couldn't justify his life's work any longer, that he had been haunted by the ghosts of the men and women he had dispatched, how they had stormed his dreams so that he had only been able to escape them by drinking so much that he obliterated all sense of his self. He told her about what had happened in East London, how he had ruined the lives of the people he had been trying to help, about how he had fled to South America and worked his way north, trying to do the right thing where he could, but moving on before he could become settled, before he could make attachments that he knew he would eventually have to break. He told her about Cuidad Juárez and Santa Muerte, about how the Group had located him and how he had escaped. He told her about San Francisco and all the dead girls and, as he did, he saw, again, that whatever he did and wherever he went, he could not escape Death. It followed in his wake, dogged and relentless and impossible to shake.

'Guilt always come to men in your work,' she said when he was finished.

'I lasted longer than most.'

'Perhaps.'

'I'm not sure what that says about me.'

She smiled, a sad smile. 'You are good man, Vanya.'

'I'm not going back.'

'You would not have that option even if you did. I am told Control is furious.'

'I'm sure he is. I put a bullet into the knee of the man he sent after me.'

'Yes, Number Twelve. His new little pet. I heard.'

'You still have your ears open?'

'I hear most things eventually. You know me.'

'That's what I was hoping. I need your help. Information.'

'Whatever I can do.'

He finished his last mouthful of blini and put the plate down on the table.

'Do you know a Colonel Shcherbatov?'

A wry half-smile. 'Pascha? I do. A little.'

'I'm meeting him tomorrow.'

'For what?'

'I'm not sure. What do you know?'

'I know that he is secretive man. He has been intelligence officer for many years. Trained with the 401st KGB School in Okhta, near St Petersburg – Leningrad, as then – and worked for Second Chief Directorate on counterintelligence and then First Chief Directorate. He monitored foreigners in Leningrad and was sent to East Germany before Wall came down. He came back to Moscow, survived coup and was given senior role in new KGB. He has been there ever since.'

'Anything else?'

'He is old-fashioned. Traditional. Still views West as enemy. He is not popular among his comrades. His views are unpopular.

Government wants good relations with West. Money from oil is worth more than principles. Pascha Shcherbatov does not share this view – old Cold Warrior. I hear suggestion that Kremlin would not be upset if he were to retire.'

'Then why didn't they get rid of him?'

'A man like Pascha learn many secrets, Vanya. He work in intelligence for many years. Do not think his attention has always been focused across Russia's borders. He is not kind of man who makes fuss of himself but apparatchiks are not stupid. They know not to be afraid of barking dog. Pascha is silent dog. You should be afraid of silent dog. Do you understand what I mean, Vanya?'

'Yes.'

'Do you know what he wants?'

'No,' Milton answered. 'I have no idea.'

'Treat him very carefully, Vanya. He is dangerous. Not to be trusted. Whatever he wants from you, it will not be good.'

18

Milton slept at the apartment that night, setting an alarm for four in the morning. He rose quietly from the couch in the hope that he might not disturb Anya Dostovalov, but she was already awake and, upon hearing that he had risen too, she bustled into the front room and made busy preparing breakfast. She prepared large mugs of Sbiten, the honey beverage laced with cloves, cinnamon and ginger, and gave one to him. She made fresh blinis and served them with sour cream. Milton didn't know when he would be eating again and so he had five of them, washing them down with another mug of Sbiten. He hugged her before opening the door, telling her that he would see her again soon, even as he knew that was unlikely, unlatched the door and stepped out into the hallway beyond.

The snow had fallen heavily overnight and walking had become even more difficult. There were huge mounds of wind-blown snow across the pavement and, where it had been cleared away, expanses of black ice. The municipal workers were out even at this early hour, preparing the city for the day ahead. They were dressed in orange overalls with thick parka jackets over the top. They shovelled snow into piles and treated patches of ice with chemicals that dissolved it with worrying hisses and fizzes.

Milton had to wait fifteen minutes for a taxi; the cold quickly robbed him of the warmth he had managed to absorb from the apartment's baking central heating and he was shivering when he finally slipped into the back seat and asked to be taken to the Ritz-Carlton.

*　*　*

Milton opened his hotel-room door quietly and slipped inside. It was just past six. He had taken off his coat and shirt and was about to run the bath when there was a knocking at the door. It was Anna. She must have been awake, listening for his return. She stood at the threshold, her arms crossed beneath her breasts. Her eyes fell to the scars on Milton's naked chest, switching back promptly as she noticed he was smiling with amusement at her.

'Where were you last night?'

'I went out.'

'Where did you go?'

'Sightseeing.'

'All night?'

'Lots of sights to see,' he said.

She frowned at him disapprovingly. 'It does you no favours to play games with us. And it does your friend no favours.'

'I'm not playing games. I'm here, aren't I? I'm ready to see the colonel.'

'Yes,' she said. 'We are leaving immediately.'

'Where is he?'

'Not in Moscow.'

'Where?'

She did not answer. 'We have a long trip ahead of us. Four hundred kilometres, Captain Milton.'

'In this snow?'

'It should take us eight hours.'

19

Milton swapped his bath for a shower, dressed warmly, and met Anna in the lobby. There was a car waiting outside for them. It was a top-of-the-line Range Rover Sport, a big and powerful four-wheel drive with snow chains fastened around all four tyres. It was black and the windows were tinted. Anna led the way to it and opened the rear door.

Milton got inside and saw that they had been provided with a driver, too. The man was dressed in an anonymous suit and his blond hair had been shaved to a short, prickly fuzz. He was an intelligence operative, he guessed, one seconded from the Spetsnaz if his guess was right. He was big, several inches taller than Milton and fifty pounds heavier. He would be armed, and tough, and a passable match for him if things took a turn for the worse. Milton looked into his face in the rear-view mirror as he slid into the seat, the man's eyes were cold and impassive as he glared back at him.

'Who's the gorilla?' he asked Anna, his eyes still fixed on the man's.

'His name is Vladimir,' she said as she slid alongside. 'He'll be driving us.'

'Just driving?'

'Don't worry, Captain Milton. You're under the protection of the Russian government now.'

'That fills me with confidence.'

'Please, relax. We have a long drive.'

'So you said. Are you going to tell me where?'

'There is a place called Plyos. North-east from here. The colonel is staying at his dacha. We will visit him there.'

'Why all the way there? You don't have a safe house in Moscow?'

'Of course we do,' she said irritably. 'But no matter how careful we are, there will always be prying eyes in the city. The colonel is a private man. Plyos is remote. A place where Muscovites go for their summer holidays. It will be deserted in this weather. There is one way in and one way out and we will be watching both. Easier for us to ensure that your meeting is not noted. That is in both our best interests, is it not?'

Milton said nothing.

The driver put the Range Rover into gear and slid into the traffic. They headed to the north.

They passed the new high-rises on the edge of Moscow and drove on. They cut into the countryside beyond, passing through picture-postcard villages that were mantled with snow. The buildings were a curious mixture of charming old houses and modern terraces, ugly and boxy. Those residents who were brave or foolish enough to be outside in the cold slouched through drifts or walked cautiously over mirror-smooth ice. There were wide lakes that must have harboured crusts of ice that were inches deep, and parked cars that had lost their shapes under the snow. They continued on, through deep forests that were garlanded with white, and, juxtaposed with the beauty, abandoned rubbish that had been dumped at the side of the road. Milton thought the landscape an apt analogy for Russia itself: the grace of years gone by that had been scarred by the ill-considered marks of progress and modernity. Goats regarded them from fields and, occasionally, they would see a wild deer or an elk. The sky was black and angry. The snow was everywhere.

They followed the E115 north, passing through Khotovo, Pereslavl-Zalessky and Rostov. Milton watched the scenery passing by the window and thought about Pope and what the Russians wanted from him. Whoever he was, Shcherbatov was obviously a man not to be taken lightly. *Mamotchka* was a tough old coot; she had seen plenty of the KGB's hardcases and blowhards, watched them rail against the unstoppable tide of capitalism, and she had outlasted them all. Her years had given her a breezy confidence and yet Milton had not missed the frown she wore throughout their discussion last night. Colonel Shcherbatov was different.

'Are you going to tell me anything about your boss?' Milton asked Anna.

'It would be better if you met him with an open mind.'

'Why? Does he have a reputation?'

'Judge him for yourself.'

The driver glanced up at him in the mirror.

'What do you think, Vladimir?'

'Colonel Shcherbatov is patriot and hero,' he said in heavily accented Russian.

'I think I'll be the judge of that.'

'You remember.'

'Vladimir,' Anna chided. 'Please. Concentrate on the road.'

*   *   *

They stopped for diesel after six hours. The station was on the outskirts of Yaroslavl, three hundred kilometres from Moscow, and Milton got out to stretch his legs. The cold grew more severe the further north they travelled and here, on the station forecourt, it took just a few minutes to spear into the marrow of his bones.

Anna got out and stood beside him, their clouded breath merging together and their shadows thrown long by the afternoon sun. They were enclosed by forest, the branches of the trees sagging with the great weight of the snow. Milton looked at the woman through the corner of his eye. She said nothing, as she had said nothing for most of the drive, but now it seemed almost a companionable silence, as if a friendship might be possible between them if the circumstances were different. He had been in the same business as her, after all. Same coin, different sides.

He absently followed her towards the garage. A wrecked, bearded man was slumped against the wall. He looked up as they approached and asked in Russian if they would buy him a bottle of vodka. Anna dismissed him curtly and went inside.

Besides the fuel, the proprietor had a ramshackle business selling beer and vodka, stationery, pornography, cigarettes, bootleg DVDs and perfume. The man glared at Milton from over the counter, a crowbar ostentatiously propped against the wall, and when he came over to the till to accept Anna's payment, he revealed an empty trouser leg that hung loose between his good leg and his crutch. He wasn't old enough for Afghanistan, Milton guessed. Chechnya.

'You smoke?' Anna said as she walked with Milton back across the forecourt to the car.

'Now and again,' he replied.

'Here.' She tossed him a packet of Winston's.

'Haven't seen these for a while,' he admitted as he tore the wrapper from the pack.

'Taste like shit and they still sell more here than anything else.'

Milton put one of the cigarettes to his lips and lit it. The tobacco was harsh and bitter and strong and he had to stifle the urge to cough.

'See what I mean?' Anna said, a half-smile brightening her face.

'It's a challenging taste,' he remarked, briefly raising an eyebrow. He mastered it and filled his lungs. 'What time will we get in?'

'Provided it doesn't snow, a few more hours.'

'And if it snows?'

'Then we'll sleep in the car.'

20

Plyos was beautiful. It had the usual Russian churches with bulbous domes. Quaint wooden houses followed a hill down to a waterfront that accommodated a fleet of charming houseboats, streetlamps glittering against the dark water. The main street might have been preserved from fifty years previously, without the designer shops that marked so many high-end Russian destinations and was blissfully free of advertising, too. Milton had visited upstate New York on several occasions, always for work, and immediately saw similarities with the Hamptons. The dacha was on the other side of the town, just outside the boundary. Large residences started to appear, walled and gated, all with plenty of land and access to the Volga.

Milton stared through the window across the vast expanse of water. It was five hundred metres wide and seventy-five metres deep, the moon throwing a rippling stripe of light across the blue-black water. A police speedboat chugged slowly across the river and, as he looked to the other side, Milton saw the signs of military activity. He knew there was no point in asking, but it was easy to guess what that meant:

a place like this, with all these big summer retreats, there had to be a good chance that members of the political elite could be found here. Oligarchs, crime lords, high-ranking military officials, all of them swimming in the money that the new Russia showered on the chosen few.

Vladimir slowed and turned off the road, stopping before a pair of gates. There were two armed guards just inside and Milton noticed the CCTV cameras that were trained down on them; after a moment, the gates parted and they continued onwards. Milton concentrated on taking in everything he could. The dacha was large, much bigger than the cabin that he had naïvely expected. They approached it along a short drive that passed through a festive Russian landscape, stands of silver birches alternating with thrusting fir and redolent pines, the greensward between them obliterated by the deep falls of snow.

There was an area for parking cars and the driver reversed next to another big executive Range Rover and an army jeep. The snow had been shovelled to the edge of the parking area, revealing the frozen gravel beneath, and as Milton stepped down from the car, he stood on a twig and snapped it, the sound ringing back through the darkness like the report from a rifle. That and the crunch of their boots on the gravel were the only sounds; everything else was muffled, as quiet as the grave.

Milton scoped out his surroundings as he allowed himself to be led to the entrance. To the south was a frozen stream, crossed, if necessary, by two planks which met at a man-made island in the middle. On the other side of the stream, and similarly set out along the banks of the Volga, were other dachas, each of them seemingly larger than the last. Milton saw smoke emerging from the chimney of the nearest one, but the rest seemed deserted. The illuminated roof and bronze cupolas of a church poked through a stand of fir. Icicles hung from the eaves of roofs, icy swords that shimmered and glimmered. The road that they had entered on was quiet. There were no other people about.

Anna had been right: this was perfect isolation. It was the ideal place to hold a meeting that no one else could know about.

Vladimir led the way to the front door. It opened on his approach and he conferred in Russian with the guard who stood behind it. The man was armed: Milton recognised his holstered weapon as an MP-443 Grach, the double-action, short-recoil 9mm that was the standard-issue Russian service pistol. The conversation was brief, and, evidently satisfied, the guard nodded and stepped aside. Vladimir waited at the door; Milton followed Anna past them both and inside.

He took it all in, unconsciously performing a tactical assessment. There was a large hallway, with doors opening out into the rest of the dacha in all three internal walls. A flight of stairs led up to a first floor and, he guessed, to a second and third above that.

Anna noticed him paying attention; she smiled and nodded at him. 'It is quite something, yes?'

She thought that he was impressed. Fair enough; he would rather she thought that than the truth, which was that he was working out the best way to breach the thick oak door.

'Who owns it?' he asked.

'The Federal Intelligence Service.'

'I saw a lot of big places as we came in.'

'Plyos is special, Captain Milton. Very exclusive.'

'And why's that?'

'Have you heard of Isaac Levitan?'

'Can't say that I have.'

Anna pointed to the wide canvas that was hung above the fireplace in the sitting room. It was a beautiful landscape, the distinctive bulbs of a Russian church reflecting against the water of a wide river. 'He was a Russian landscape painter. Very famous. He worked here. He painted it many times. That is one of his works.'

'I'm not great with art.'

She ignored that. 'Many famous artists have been drawn here. It is very beautiful in the daylight.'

'Shame we're not here to visit, then.'

'Yes. There will be no time for sightseeing, not like in Moscow.'

He ignored the jibe and allowed her to lead the way upstairs. They reached a landing with several doors leading from it; again, Milton committed the layout to memory. Anna took him halfway down and pushed one of the doors ajar.

'This is your room,' she said.

Milton opened the door fully and looked inside. It was a large room, dominated by a four-poster bed. It was furnished with heavy linens and had a brick stove beneath a marble fireplace. A fire had been made, and, as the flames curled around the logs that had been stacked there, they cast their orange and yellow light into the dark corners. It was warm and friendly.

'Please, stay here tonight. There's nothing to see in the village after dark and there are armed guards posted outside. They have been told to prevent you from leaving. I'm sure you could avoid them, but it wouldn't do you any favours. The temperature up here is colder than in Moscow. If you don't have the right clothes, and you don't, you wouldn't last twenty minutes. Much better to stay here, where it's warm. Okay?'

'Don't worry,' Milton said. 'I'm not going anywhere.'

Anna nodded her approval. 'The cook will prepare anything you like for your dinner. It will be brought to your room.' She indicated the telephone next to the bed with a nod of her head. 'You just need to dial 1 to speak to the kitchen.'

Milton stepped further into the room, sat on the edge of the bed and started to work his boots off.

Anna stayed at the door. 'The colonel is arriving tomorrow morning. He wants to see you immediately. We will have breakfast together and then I will introduce you.'

'I'll look forward to it.'

Her face softened with the beginnings of a careful smile. 'My room is next door. If you need anything, you only need knock.'

She said it as she stared into his face; it was meant to be meaningful, and Milton did not mistake the message.

He was tempted, but he did not take the bait. 'Thank you,' he said. 'In the morning, then.'

If she was offended, she didn't show it. 'Sleep well, Captain Milton,' she said, closing the door. 'You have a big day tomorrow.'

*   *   *

Milton was awoken by the sound of an engine. He reached out for his watch: the luminous dial showed a little after three. He slipped out of bed and, crossing the room quietly, reached the window and parted the thick blackout curtains. Snow was falling heavily outside, fat flakes that had already piled two inches deep against the sill and limited the view to a handful of metres.

Milton saw headlights approaching from the road, an amber glow that moved slowly through the blizzard. A large, Humvee-style vehicle painted in military camouflage drew into the parking space and reversed to a halt so that its rear doors faced the dacha. Milton recognised the vehicle as a GAZ 2975 Tigr: large, heavily treaded tyres, an armoured cabin and narrow windows at the front, rear and along each flank. Troop transport, for the most part, and rugged enough to make short work of this weather. The engine cut out and the driver and passenger-side doors opened. Two soldiers disembarked, crunched across the compacted snow to the rear and opened the doors. The driver hauled himself up into the back and emerged with a third man. He looked half-unconscious, falling to one knee as his feet hit the ground.

The two men put his arms across their shoulders and dragged him into the dacha. Milton's view was from above and obscured by the wide flanks of the Tigr and the falling snow, but he saw enough of the man's face to recognise Captain Michael Pope.

21

Mamotchka knew plenty about Colonel Pavel Valerievich Shcherbatov. He had first been called Pascha when he was a little boy; it was the diminutive of his forename and it had stuck with him ever since. For a man in his position of authority, it might have been assumed by his juniors that the formal approach would be appropriate, but Shcherbatov's reputation went before him and he had found that he could afford to give the impression of avuncularity; no one who knew anything about him could have been confused about the consequences of taking advantage of his good nature. He was an amiable man, prone to laughter, and his easy smile had carved deep lines from the corners of his mouth and around his eyes. But he was a cunning man, an operator of the highest order, and those eyes shone with a wary intelligence that was impossible to miss. He was also ruthless and without scruple. It was difficult to advance in the Russian intelligence service without those qualities.

Shcherbatov was sixty-two and in excellent shape. He ran five miles around the SVR's indoor track in Yasenevo every morning and made it his habit to complete at least one marathon a year;

he could still cover the Moscow course in under four hours. His exertions had kept him trim and supple. One of his few weaknesses was vanity, and that he could still turn the heads of the women under his command was important to him. He was not wearing his uniform when he came into the room where Milton and Anna were waiting for him. He was wearing a black sweater and jeans.

'Captain Milton,' he said. 'I am Pavel Valerievich Shcherbatov. It is good to meet you.'

He extended his hand and, after a short pause, Milton took it. His shake was firm and Milton could feel how powerful his grip could be; it was a strangler's grip.

'I admit I know much about you, Captain. You can be sure I will not underestimate you.'

Milton held onto his hand for a moment longer than was necessary and then let go.

Shcherbatov smiled at that, unfazed. 'We have Department of Analysis and Information in Moscow. They have attributed many deaths to you. I have worked with the most dangerous assassins in Russian Federation and, before that, Soviet Union. You are as dangerous as any of them.'

Milton shrugged off the praise. 'I'm afraid I don't know very much about you, Colonel.'

'Call me Pascha,' he said. 'Please. No need for formality.'

'That's all right. I'd prefer colonel, if you don't mind.'

'Very well, Captain Milton. But I must ask: are you sure you do not know me?'

Milton looked at him again. 'No, sir. I'm afraid I don't.'

'Your memory is poor, Captain Milton. You do not remember our previous meeting? Surely, eight years is not so long that you would forget?'

Now he did pause and Shcherbatov noticed his renewed interest.

'Why don't you help me out?' Milton suggested.

'In career, how many targets escaped you?'

'Not many,' Milton said, although he had made the connection now. 'There was one, right at the start.'

'I believe I am fortunate enough to say I am only man you were sent to kill who got away.' Shcherbatov smiled benignly at him as he sat. 'We were going to see your Control. You and another agent attacked car. I escaped. You did not shoot me. Do you remember now?'

'I never knew your name,' Milton said.

'I am sure you did not. I believe I was SNOW. My companion, Anastasia Ivanovna Semenko, was DOLLAR. She was not as fortunate.'

Milton flexed, sensing the unsaid threat in Shcherbatov's words.

'Do not concern yourself, Captain. I do not seek revenge – at least not from you. You were following orders. You are soldier. I understand how that works.'

Milton didn't relax. 'So why am I here?'

'Because I have something for you to do.'

Milton shook his head. 'I'm sorry, Colonel. I'm out of the game. I'm not interested.'

'Then I must ask you – why did you come?'

'I didn't have a choice.' He turned to Anna. 'Your comrade dragged me here; she says you have a friend of mine.'

'Indeed we do. Captain Pope.'

'That's right. I came to persuade you to release him.'

'Perhaps. But we need you to do something for us first.'

'I don't—'

Shcherbatov raised his hands to interrupt him. 'You have retired. We know this. But it is not a violent thing. We want you to find something for us. Information. You can get it.'

'What information?'

'In good time, Captain Milton.' He turned to the girl. 'Anna Vasil'yevna Kushchyenko—you leave us now, please.'

'Yes, Colonel,' she said, dipping her head and then exiting the room, closing the door behind her.

'I hope she treated you with respect, Captain Milton. We do respect you. Your work is well known to us.' Shcherbatov got up, took a log from the store and dropped it onto the fire. 'Your friend, Control, has he ever mentioned me?'

Milton shrugged. 'Why would he?'

'Because he and I know each other very well.'

Milton shook his head. 'If he has, I don't recall it.'

'Let me tell you story, Captain Milton. Many years ago, I travel to London for interesting assignment. I am sent with female agent, Anastasia Ivanovna Semenko. It is proposed that we pose as couple. She is to work as independent contractor in arms industry, I am lawyer. I land in London, find flat, establish necessary contacts. Nastya joins me and we grow close. What was supposed to be fiction became truth. It is inevitable, yes, you must have experienced this?'

Milton eyed him, steely, said nothing.

'The interesting assignment: Russian intelligence has suggested that there is senior English spy who is vulnerable to blackmail. We hear from colleagues in Tehran and Baghdad that he has sold information to both regimes. He sells information to Israel, too. The man is venal, so they tell us. So we think perhaps we can trap this man, use him for our purposes?'

Shcherbatov stood close enough so that the fire could warm his legs. Milton watched him hawkishly.

'This official – I see you realise it is your Control. Nastya make contact with him through intermediary. She say she has transaction to put to Damascus, but she is finding difficulty in proving she is' – he searched for the right word – 'legitimate. Control say that he can arrange introduction. He vouch for Nastya, in return for percentage of deal, of course.'

Milton kept on staring at him.

'All the time, we are gathering evidence. He is very careful. No phone calls, no emails. But we build case against him. We have photographs of him meeting Nastya. We can demonstrate payment of funds he demands. Eventually, we have enough to demonstrate good sense in his working with us. Alternative would not be good for him. There is meeting. He is surprised to learn he has been tricked and it does not go well. There is a second meeting. It goes better. He says he will think about proposal. We make progress, I think, and then he suggest third meeting to discuss matter properly. It is to be on Embankment. Next to river and Houses of Parliament. You know the rest, Captain Milton. My Nastya is killed and I am fortunate to escape.' He smiled as he spoke, the smile of a friendly uncle. It was a practised expression, the instant smile of a politician or a salesman, a mask to hide his true feelings. It was a good mask, honed by experience, but Shcherbatov could not disguise the glitter of hatred in his eyes. 'Ever since then,' he continued, 'I watch his career. And I wait.'

Milton frowned. 'You had the evidence against him. Why not use it?'

'We lost evidence. We have copies of photographs, of course, but they are insufficient on their own. A man and a woman meeting in a park. What is that? We had financial information on portable drives, but they were taken when we were attacked.'

Milton scowled dubiously. 'You didn't back it up?'

'Of course. But Control sent other agents to take back-ups. Four Russian agents killed, evidence lost. God takes care of man who takes care of himself, Captain, and Control is clever man.' He put his hands together and steepled his fingers. 'There is Russian proverb: "every seed knows its time." I have waited years for chance to settle old score. Now I have that chance. Can you see why I wanted to speak to you now? You are perfect. He hates you. You hate him. I hate him. We have something in common.'

'I doubt that.'

'Control is common enemy. We have similar experience. We know he is ruthless. He has taken things that are important to us. My Nastya. Your liberty.'

Shcherbatov was still standing, the flames still warming his legs, and he looked down at Milton, unmoving in the armchair. There was a set of antique Russian dolls on the mantelpiece and the colonel took the smallest and turned it between his thumb and forefinger.

'You haven't told me what you want me to do,' Milton said.

'We have found someone who has information we lost. You will acquire it. We will put information into public domain and result will be his disgrace. He must be humiliated. And then, when he has been stripped of everything,' he snapped his fingers, 'then you know what comes next. We have our own cleaners, as you know.'

'Even if I could get the information, why would I do it?'

'Maybe you talk to Captain Pope. Ask him what he thinks.'

22

Shcherbatov led the way into the hallway and then through a narrow archway, down a flight of stone steps.

The temperature dropped quickly away from the warmth of the fire. The stairs were dank and the steps were slick with frozen mildew and Milton braced himself with one hand against the icy stone wall. They reached what he guessed was the cellar and Shcherbatov pulled down on a drawstring, lighting the single naked bulb that was suspended overhead. Milton blinked at the light, taking in the medium-sized room. It was constructed in the foundations of the dacha, maybe four metres wide and five metres long, with rough stone walls and a concrete floor. The bulb was the only illumination and it wasn't strong enough to dispel the shadows around the edges of the room. Metal bars had been fitted halfway into it, flush to the floor and the ceiling and reaching all the way across. The ironwork looked substantial. There was a doorway in the middle of the bars, the door secured with a bolt that was itself fastened by an industrial padlock.

Milton took a step forward.

The cell, for that was what it was, was furnished with a simple cot and a bucket. The cot was covered with a dirty blanket and, beneath that, Milton could make out the shape of a man's body.

'I leave you to talk, Captain Milton. Come upstairs after.'

Milton turned to Shcherbatov, but he was already climbing back to the ground floor.

Milton paused at the edge of the cage and looked at the man inside. He was lying towards him and, even in the dim light, and with the shadowed grid from the bars that fell across his face, Milton recognised Michael Pope.

'Pope,' he said. 'Pope, wake up.'

The man stirred on the cot.

'Wake up, Pope.'

'Who is it?' His voice was weak and uncertain.

'It's Milton.'

'Who?'

'John Milton.'

'What?'

'It's me, Pope. Come on, wake up.'

'Milton?' Pope repeated, his voice sluggish and slurred, as if his mouth had been stuffed full of cotton wool. 'What? What are you doing here?'

'I'm going to get you out.'

Pope didn't register that. 'Didn't expect to see you again.'

'Wasn't planning on it. Not after last time.'

He chuckled: a weak, low sound. 'Sorry about that.' He made a whooping, hacking sound that Milton guessed was an attempt at laughter.

The last time. Nearly seven months ago in Ciudad Juárez, Mexico, Pope had led the team that had been sent to track him down and bring him back. The orders had been equivocal about how they did that, dead or alive, and Pope had intervened to prevent Callan from making sure his return flight was in a body bag.

Milton stepped right up to the bars and took one in each hand. Pope shuffled around so that he could lower his legs to the floor and he sat up, slowly and unsteadily. The light fell on him more evenly and Milton could see the damage that the Russians had done. He had been badly beaten: his right eye was swollen shut and his left was blackened; there was a purple welt all the way down the side of his face, striated with the pattern that the sole of a boot might make; his chin had been split open and sutured back together again in a quick and ugly fashion.

'How'd I look?' he said.

'Not great,' Milton admitted. 'How'd you manage to get in a mess like this?'

'Shouldn't have happened, should it? Got sloppy.'

Milton yanked at the bars as hard as he could: they were fitted well and there was no give in them at all. 'You think?'

Pope held a hand up against the contusions on his face and smiled ruefully through the wince of pain. 'He tell you what happened?'

'Just that they arrested you. What were you doing?'

He took in a deep breath, as if steeling himself. His voice, when it came again, was reedy and soft. 'Control sent me after him.'

'Shcherbatov?'

Slowly and with evident pain, Pope stood and walked to the bars. Each step forced an exhalation of pain. 'He was in Monaco.'

Milton hushed him and pointed up to the ceiling.

'They're recording all right,' Pope said. 'But no need to worry, I told them everything already.' He laughed again, and then coughed some more. 'So I got the file. Don't know what went wrong. The infiltration . . . all messed up. They were waiting for me. Took me somewhere, knocked me out. Then I'm in a concrete room in the Lubyanka, strapped to a table with a bag over my head.' He coughed again, hacking hard. 'Don't worry. I'm okay.'

'You don't look it.'

'What's a little waterboarding between friends?'

Milton looked at him anxiously. He wasn't okay. Far from it. Every cough seemed to end with him swallowing back fluid, as if his lungs were waterlogged. He was feverish, sweating and shivering simultaneously. Milton had seen plenty of men with pneumonia and that was what it looked like to him. Christ, he thought. Pneumonia. If he had that, he wouldn't survive a week in the north.

'What about you?' Pope wheezed out. 'What are you doing here?'

Milton told him about his arrest, about Anna breaking him out and about the proposition she had put to him. 'You need to keep it together, Pope,' he said when he was finished. 'I'm going to get you out.'

'Don't be an idiot, John. That's not your job any more.'

'What else am I going to do? Leave you to rot?'

Pope looked at him, his eyes burning beneath their rheumy film. 'You leave it to the diplomats. I do a little time, they swap me for someone we nabbed that they want back. You know how it works. You can't do anything,' he coughed, 'and we both know you can't trust them.'

'I know that. But I can listen.'

'To what?'

'To what he has to say.'

23

Shcherbatov watched as Milton came back into the sitting room; it was almost dizzily warm compared to the frigid cellar. A silver platter had been left out on the table: a teapot, a samovar of hot water and two cups. The civility was a stark contrast with the cold and the darkness below. Milton knew that Shcherbatov was making a point: it had been necessary to take him down there in order to underline it. Pope's future would be unpleasant and short if he did not co-operate.

Shcherbatov poured tea into the cups and topped it up with hot water from the samovar. He left a cup on the table within Milton's reach and took his to the opposite armchair.

'Do you like tea, Captain Milton? It an English passion, yes? This is Russian Caravan blend: oolong, keemun and lapsang souchong. It has malty, smoky taste. Very nice, I think.' Shcherbatov sipped his tea carefully, watching Milton over the lip of the cup.

'He's ill,' Milton said. 'He has pneumonia.'

'He will be cared for.'

'Like you've cared for him already?'

Shcherbatov waved that off. 'He will be cared for *properly*. You have my word.'

'Nothing happens to him,' Milton said.

'Or?'

'Let's leave that unsaid, shall we? I'd rather be civil. But you know what I'm capable of.'

Shcherbatov smiled his best, conciliatory smile. 'I understand you are angry, Captain Milton, but there is no need. We are friends. You help us, he is returned to you.'

'Who is it you want me to find?'

'Member of team responsible for the attack. Intelligence says this agent has means and opportunity to assist. We want you to find agent, find proof of Control's corruption, and bring proof to us. If you do that, Captain Pope will be released. If not' – he spread his arms and left a pause – 'if not, Captain Milton, your friend has unhappy stay in Siberia.'

'Who is the agent?'

'Her name is Beatrix Rose. At the time of attack, she was Number One.'

Milton's eyes narrowed and he clenched his jaw; Shcherbatov noticed.

'And you know where she is?' Milton asked.

'We do,' Shcherbatov confirmed. 'Hong Kong.'

24

The taxi drew up to the rank outside the terminal at Sheremetyevo airport. Milton got out and collected his new suitcase from the boot. It had been waiting in his room for him, together with its contents, when he had returned to the Ritz-Carlton after the long drive back south yesterday afternoon. There was another new suit, three plain white shirts, underwear, two new pairs of shoes.

He'd had a little time to kill and he would have appreciated the chance to speak to Anya Dostovalov again, but he'd decided against it. He had lost his tail easily enough the first time around, and it would be tempting fate to think that they would not have augmented his detail now, especially since he knew now what they wanted him to do. He was not prepared to risk compromising her anonymity just to salve his unease. Instead, he had done as he was told: he had stayed in his room, ordered room service and was in bed and asleep by eleven. He had a feeling he might need his sleep.

Anna Vasil'yevna Kushchyenko was waiting for him inside the terminal.

'What are you doing here?' Milton asked.

'I'm coming with you.'

'That's not a good idea.'

'It's not up for discussion. The colonel wants me to come.'

'To keep an eye on me?'

'You can understand that he doesn't trust you, Captain?'

'You'll get in my way. You'll make it more difficult.'

'We'll just have to manage.'

Milton thought about insisting, but he knew there was little point. If she had a ticket for the same plane to Hong Kong that he did, there would be nothing he could do to stop her getting onto it. It would be easier to get rid of her on the other side.

* * *

The Russians had bought him a first-class ticket. Air Astana 929's itinerary called for two stops in Kazakhstan en route to Hong Kong: the first after three hours in Astana and the second, after another two hours, in Almaty. The plane was an Airbus A320 and, thankfully, it looked like it was in decent condition.

Milton's seat was on the aisle, with Anna opposite him. He stared out of the porthole as the plane accelerated away down the runway, climbing into the angry black sky that had remained over Moscow since their arrival. The vast city, covered over with white, disappeared from view as they climbed into the dark clouds and then, after fifteen minutes, they broke through into the clear vault of midnight blue above.

The stewardess, statuesque and with the Asiatic cheekbones and complexion of a typical Eastern European beauty,

126

pushed the trolley down the aisle, the bottles clinking with their promise of oblivion. Milton hadn't been to a meeting since he had left San Francisco and he felt the familiar temptation even more keenly than usual. The bottles rattled joyfully, the stewardess bending closer to his head and asking whether she could get him anything. Milton looked at the miniatures of gin, whisky, and vodka for longer than he had for months, but, when she asked him again, he shook his head. When she left, he found that he was gripping the armrests so tightly that his knuckles were white.

A moment later, he realised he was about to have the dream again. The first time in months. He closed his eyes, trying to control his breathing, the urge to gasp and gulp, focusing everything to keep it inside, keep it hidden so that Anna – close enough to touch if he reached out an arm – didn't see his weakness. That familiar feeling of fatigue, of being hollowed out, like a beaker into which misery and pain would be poured. Milton felt the muscles in his shoulders lock and set, as if petrified, and then his thighs and his calves. He held onto the armrests again. Then he was gone, barely conscious, standing in a blasted desert, the heat rising from the sand in woozy waves, and the smell of high explosives cloying in his nostrils. Time passed; he had no idea how long. He heard a lone, anguished cry and it sounded so strange because he should have been alone in the desert, but then he turned and it all flooded over him.

The desert.
The village.
The madrasa.

'Captain Milton?'

The children in their Western football strips.

The plastic football, jerking in the wind.

'Captain Milton?'

The young boy.

The plane, fast and low, engines echoing through the valley.

'John?'

He followed the sound of the voice out of the dream, forcing himself out of the desert and back into the cabin of the jet: the endless drone of the engines, the clink of cutlery on china plates, the sound of a baby crying in the back of the plane.

'John?'

He turned to Anna and forced a smile onto his face.

'You were moaning, Captain Milton.'

'Bad dream,' he said. 'Sleeping tablet. Must have disagreed with me. What time is it?'

'Eleven.'

They had been in the air for three hours.

'Are you sure you're all right? You missed your meal.'

She looked at him and, for a moment, he wondered if there was something on her face beyond the dutiful concern of an intelligence agent responsible for the well-being of an important asset. Her hair shimmered in the shining cone of the overhead light, her green eyes glittered.

'I'm fine,' he said. 'Not hungry.' He reclined his seat until it was flat and covered himself with the thin blanket that the airline supplied. 'Get some sleep. We're going to be busy tomorrow.'

PART 4

HONG KONG

25

Hong Kong tended to enjoy dry winters; the guidebooks all suggested that the autumn was one of the better times to visit, with pleasant temperatures and dry days.

As the Airbus descended from thirty thousand feet, however, it passed through a deep carpet of cloud that became progressively darker and angrier until it was almost pitch black outside the windows. The rain, as they sank into it, was a deluge, a torrential flood that had hammered on the city for three days and showed no sign of abating. The pilot came over the intercom and did his best to reassure his passengers that, although they were in for a bumpy landing, it was not unusual for Chek Lap Kok.

His words did not go very far and, as the plane started to be buffeted by powerful gusts of wind and the rain sheeted against the windows, several passengers closed their eyes and clasped their hands and prayed to whatever deity they thought would protect them. Milton had been to Hong Kong six times before and had been there long enough ago to remember the old airport, Kai Tak, where jumbos seemingly aimed at the ramshackle apartments blocks before banking at the last minute to line up for the approach to the runway. In comparison, a bit of nasty weather at Chek Lap Kok was nothing to get too worked up about.

The details of the new facility resolved from out of the rain-lashed murk: the reclaimed land, the hangars, the servicing areas, the jumbos lined up at the terminal building and then the runway, demarcated by arrays of red and yellow lights. The plane bumped as it descended, the rear wheels screeched as they bit into the asphalt, the front wheel followed, and the reverse thrusters roared as the plane's headlong rush was arrested.

Milton packed away the book he had been reading and allowed his thoughts to wander a little.

Beatrix Rose: that was a name he hadn't heard for many years.

She had disappeared after the botched operation to assassinate DOLLAR and SNOW; or, as he knew now, Pascha Shcherbatov and Anastasia Ivanovna Semenko. There had been nothing from Control that might have explained her absence, but that, in itself, was not unusual. Group operations were typically one- or two-member jobs and, even where Milton had been paired with another, it was usually a different agent each time. Group Fifteen was carefully segmented so that each agent was independent of all the others. It was their own form of the cut-out that had shielded the agents who worked with *Mamotchka*; should one of them be captured, it would not matter how badly they were tortured since they would not know anything about the other members of the

Group. Everyone breaks eventually during torture; it is a simple matter of biology. But you cannot reveal details that you do not know.

Milton knew a little more about Beatrix because she had presided over his selection and training, but, even then, his knowledge was limited. He did not know very much about her private or professional lives, where she lived, what she had done before she joined the Group. He did not know her politics, her likes or dislikes, anything that might allow him to dab a little colour on the empty tracing of her personality. He did know that she was a brilliant agent, terrifyingly clear in her focus and relentless when she had been given a target. Of all of the men and women he had worked with during his career with Group Fifteen, Beatrix Rose, who would always be Number One in his eyes, was the most impressive by far.

He realised now, as he remembered her, that he had never really given the question of her disappearance much thought, save her luck must have run out during a job. That happened. But now that he knew that she was alive, and hiding in a place like this, he began to wonder. He had experience of Control's ruthlessness. He had form for seeking to terminate his top agent when he lost his trust in him. It did not seem so far-fetched, especially given what Shcherbatov had told him, that he had done the same to her.

Milton looked out at the multitude of lights that twinkled amid the throbbing power of the storm. Finding a person in a city like this, an abundance of millions crammed onto an island that was much too small for them, was going to be difficult. He hoped that the leads that Shcherbatov had uncovered were enough.

The plane drew up to the gate and the pilot extinguished the Fasten Seat Belts sign. Across the aisle, Anna stood up and muscled her carry-on luggage down from the overhead bin.

'Here we are,' Anna said.

'Here we are.'

Their passports recorded them as Mr and Mrs Roberts. For the purposes of their cover story, they were a couple from London in Hong Kong for a vacation. Milton had questioned whether Anna's accent would raise suspicion, but she modulated it effortlessly: the light southwestern twang that she used while in America had been superseded by a more guttural Russian inflection while they were in Moscow and now, that, in turn, had been replaced by a flatness that could very easily have located her in the English Home Counties. She was an excellent chameleon.

They followed the snake of passengers down the aisle and disembarked onto the air bridge. As the corridor widened, Anna moved alongside him and slipped her hand in his. Milton did not resist.

26

They made it through immigration with no issues and took a taxi to the city centre. Anna asked their driver for the Landmark Mandarin and he piloted them through the drenched streets, the tail lights of the cars ahead of them smeared as stripes of red against the sodden tarmac. Milton looked out of the window, reminding himself of the city: everything was tight and cramped, the skyscrapers jostling each other shoulder to shoulder, the buildings sheathed in black glass. They reflected the vast neon signs that flicked between advertisements: a pretty Asian girl, all perfect skin and red lips and gleaming teeth, selling insurance; an SUV, too bulky for these choked roads; confectionery and instant noodles and gambling websites and catwalk models and more cars and online catalogues. The streets were crammed and hectic.

The Mandarin was an expensive, luxury hotel. The reception was neat and functional and the girl behind the desk processed their reservation with good-natured efficiency. Only as they exited the lift on the fifteenth floor did Milton pause to consider their sleeping arrangements. They were husband and wife; their cover demanded that they share the same room.

Anna approached the door and slid the card key into the reader. She must have detected his unease and, pausing in the doorway, she put a hand on his arm. 'It's a twin room,' she said, standing aside so that he could see into the large room. 'Our cover need not extend any further than this.' She left her hand across his bicep and he knew what she was leaving unsaid: *unless you want it to.*

'This will be fine,' he said.

Milton stepped inside and, unable to suppress the caution that had been drilled into him over the course of a decade, hundreds of nights spent in identical rooms like this in countries where the local spooks made it a matter of routine to bug arriving travellers, he made a quick examination: the generous en suite with a bath and shower; the twin beds; the large LCD screen on the bureau; the telephone beside the bed.

He went back to the start and made a more detailed inspection. He dropped to his knees and checked under the beds, then he took out a dime from his pocket and used it to unscrew the plug sockets. He removed the bulbs from the lights and dismantled the telephone handset. He opened the wardrobe, lifted the television from the desk and shut it away. It took him ten minutes to satisfy himself that everything was as it should be. Anna watched him quietly, saying nothing.

Milton wheeled his bag to the furthest bed, stood by the window and looked out. The window was high up and the view was impressive. The swarm of people in the street below hurried about their business, their umbrellas like tiny black mushrooms. The skyscrapers bristled, utilitarian and graceless, the tops muffled by low clouds. Lightning forked the sky and, seconds later, the answering boom of thunder rattled the glass in the window.

Seven million people, Milton thought.

He sat down on the edge of the bed, unable to ignore the fatigue that had sunk into his muscles and bones.

Seven million.

The sheer weight of the number pressed down on him oppressively. He had to find one person amid the mad tumult. That person, for all he knew, had been hiding in the city for years; hiding successfully, too, which was more than he could say for himself. Control and the Group had located him in just six months and the Russians had found him again soon after that. Beatrix Rose was better than he was. If she didn't want to be found, Milton wouldn't find her.

'When will you start?' Anna asked him.

Milton assessed his reserves of energy. The dream had exhausted him, as it always did, and the task could wait another day.

'Tomorrow,' he said.

He took off his shoes and shirt and went through into the bathroom. He closed the door, undressed and stood beneath the shower for twenty minutes, scrubbing the hot water into his scalp. He dried himself and pulled on the dressing gown embossed with the hotel's logo. He stood before the mirror and regarded himself carefully. He did not inspect himself because of vanity, although pride would have been warranted if he was so inclined. He did so because he was an artisan; his body was his tool and his discipline demanded that it was always in good condition. The horizontal scar on his face seemed to have faded a little, as if blanched by the chill of Moscow, and the tattoo across his shoulders and back was more obvious now that his tan had faded.

He opened the door and went back into the bedroom. Anna had undressed, her clothes folded neatly on top of her suitcase. She was in bed, her chest rising and falling with the shallow susurration of her breath. Milton watched her sleeping: the long red hair; the full lips; the vulnerable, exposed neck; the slim body with the shape of her breasts perfectly obvious beneath the thin cotton sheet; the curve of her hip; the long legs; the porcelain white, ice-pale, skin. He wondered, for a moment, whether he could allow himself the luxury of accepting her unspoken and yet obvious offer.

No, he decided. *He could not.*

He crossed the room quietly, removed the dressing gown and slid between the cool sheets of the other bed. He closed his eyes, listening to the hum of the air conditioning and the exhalations of her breath.

27

Milton couldn't sleep.

His mind was turning this way and that and there was nothing that he could do to settle it. He got up and made his way quietly across the room to the chair where he had piled his clothes. He took them into the bathroom and dressed, took one of the key cards from the writing desk, left the room and took the lift down to the lobby.

There was a small business centre just away from the main desk with a couple of Macs, a fax machine and a printer. One of the computers was occupied and so Milton sat down next to the other one, opened the web browser and navigated to Google. He found the information he wanted, closed the browser down, cleared the history and went outside.

It was still hot and humid, steam issuing from air vents and from the grates in the street. There was a taxi rank next to the hotel and he nodded to the driver of the one at the front of the queue; he nudged his car forwards and Milton got inside.

'Where to, sir?'

'Connaught Road West,' Milton said. 'Sai Ying Pun.'

'Yes, sir.'

It was midnight. Milton had not been particularly surprised to find that there was an English-speaking meeting, even at this hour. Hong Kong was a twenty-four-hour city, after all, and being a drunk was a twenty-four-hour problem. It was a closed meeting, which meant that only those in the fellowship were able to attend, and its title was 'Humble in HK'.

Milton had not been to a meeting for weeks and he knew that he made himself more vulnerable to the dream every extra day he missed. That, in turn, made him more vulnerable to the temptation of taking a first drink, and everything he had learned in the months he had spent in the Rooms, all the way through South America and in San Francisco, made one thing perfectly clear: he would not stop at the first drink.

Connaught Road was a flyover that passed through an unlovely area of town in the Central District. Tall office buildings were to the left and a stretch of park was to the right. The driver exited the flyover and looped back around so that he could get to the maze of roads that ran beneath it.

Po Fung Mansion was a three-storey building with a shuttered takeaway on the ground floor. It was constructed from concrete and its walls were adorned with air-conditioning units, a metal balustrade that prevented a drop from the first-floor balcony and a collection of unhealthy-looking potted plants.

Traffic hummed across the flyover and the three-lane road beneath it. It was busy, smoky and noisy, and the three young men loitering outside the entrance to the nearby bar glared dolefully at Milton as he stepped out of the car. He paid the man and the taxi drove off. The men kept looking; Milton ignored them. He saw the familiar sign blowing in the breeze, attached with a piece of string to the door handle: two blue As, within a triangle, within a circle.

He crossed the street, opened the door and went up to the third floor.

*   *   *

The meeting had just started: the secretary had welcomed the group and was about to lead them in the Serenity Prayer. He smiled at Milton and indicated an empty seat in the front row. Milton felt self-conscious as he picked his way towards it and sat down gratefully.

The secretary recited the prayer: 'God, give me the serenity to accept the things I cannot change, courage to change the things I can, and wisdom to know the difference.'

He continued with the familiar preamble and introduced the member who had been asked to read from the Big Book. Milton closed his eyes and listened, gratefully aware that the tension and worry was seeping out of him.

The reader finished and closed the book.

'Do we have any new members tonight?' the secretary asked.

No one raised their hand.

'Any visitors?'

There was no point in staying silent; they all knew he was fresh at the meeting. 'My name is John and I'm an alcoholic,' he said. 'I'm from London.'

The others returned the greeting, welcoming him.

The secretary introduced the speaker. The man's name was Chuck. He was corpulent: he dressed in a white shirt and beige trousers and he talked in a lazy American drawl. He didn't discuss his background in depth, but Milton gathered that he was stationed in the city on behalf of an American corporation. His story was about the things he had done as a younger man; he did not specify exactly what they were, fencing around the subject even in light of the injunction that members should not fear honesty, but it was obvious that something had happened with his family and that it still caused him great shame.

Milton closed his eyes again and allowed the man's words to wash over him. The precise content of the story was not important (it involved a series of domestic faults that this man had to regret) and it could not have been more different to the bloody crimes that haunted Milton's dreams. The point of a good share was to find the similarities and not the differences, and Milton understood the man's disgrace, his insecurity, and the fear that he would never be able to atone for his sins. Those were the universal similarities that bonded all of them together; the details didn't matter.

Chuck finished and the secretary opened the floor. There was a long pause and, smiling, the secretary turned to Milton. 'How about our visitor?' he said. 'Care to share back?'

Milton cleared his throat. 'Thank you for your share,' he said.

Chuck acknowledged him with a duck of his head and, for a moment, Milton wondered whether he had said enough. He remembered the advice of his first sponsor, the man who had taken him under his wing at the first meeting he had attended in London: you had to share, he had advised him. It was the only way to draw the sting of the toxic thoughts that would inevitably lead to drink.

The others were waiting to see if he was going to continue; he cleared his throat and went on. 'I'm not from Hong Kong. Just here on business, stopping for a couple of days and then moving on, but I really needed a meeting tonight. I'm very grateful to have found it.'

'And we're glad you did too,' said the secretary.

'I don't really know what I want to talk about. I suppose it is partly about gratitude. I'm grateful to you for being here, I'm grateful to the fellowship for giving me the tools that I need to quieten my mind, and I'm grateful that my life has been returned to me. I have a lot of things in my past to regret and this has been the only thing I have ever found that gives me peace. Saying that, I haven't been to a meeting for days. It's the longest I've been without one throughout my sobriety and I don't mind admitting that it has shown me that I'm very far from being cured. I've been struggling with memories from my past and with the temptation to drink so that I can forget them. I couldn't sleep tonight and I was close to going into the hotel bar and ordering a gin. If this meeting hadn't been here, maybe that's what I would have done. But it was, and I didn't, and after listening to your story, I know that I won't drink, at least not tonight. Day by day, right? That's what we say. We just take it a day at a time.' He paused again. He felt better, the stress that had twisted in his shoulders dissipating with every word. 'Well,' he said. 'That's it. Thank you. I think that's what I wanted to say.'

It was one in the morning when the meeting finished and the others explained that they usually went for noodles at a late-night restaurant that was around the corner. Milton thanked them for the offer but politely declined. He wanted to have a little time to himself. The hotel was on the other side of the island.

He decided that he would walk.

28

Milton's thoughts reached back; years ago, although it still felt like yesterday. He would usually do anything to think of something else, because the memory was the foundation for the dream. As he walked along the harbour front, he allowed himself to remember.

Milton and Pope were in the middle of the desert. It was blisteringly hot, the air quivering so that it looked as if they were gazing through the water in an aquarium, and he could still remember the woozy dizziness of being broiled in the sun for so long. It was Iraq, at the start of the invasion, and their eight-man SAS patrol was deep behind Saddam's lines. There was some suggestion that the madman was readying his army to fling scuds tipped with nerve gas into Israel and the patrol's instructions were to set up observation posts, find the launchers and disable them.

A Chinook had dropped them and a second patrol, together with their Land Rovers and eighty-pound Bergens, into the desert between Baghdad and north-western Iraq. They had been given a wide swathe of territory to patrol. They found one launcher within the first three days; they had killed the crew, slapped a pound of plastique on the fuel tank and blown the equipment to high heaven.

They ranged north after that, travelling at night and hiding out during the day, and eventually they had picked up the scent of another crew. They had tracked them to a village fifty clicks east of Al-Qa'im. It was a small settlement dependent on goat herding, just a collection of huts set around a tiny madrasa. The soldiers were elite, Republican Guard, and they were smart. Their launcher was an old Soviet R-11 and they had driven it right into the middle of the settlement, parking next to the school and obscuring the vehicle beneath a camo net. The thinking was obvious: if they were discovered, surely the Americans would think twice about launching a missile into the middle of a civilian area, much less at a target that was next to a school?

They had found an escarpment five hundred yards to the west of the village and settled in to reconnoitre. They would wait where they were until either one of two things had happened: either the launcher abandoned its hiding place and moved out, in which case they would take it down with a LAW missile once it was out of range of the village, or, if it stayed where it was, they would wait until sunset to go in and take out the crew. Those options, as far as Milton was concerned, were the only ones that would remove the risk of civilian casualties.

He used the HF radio to send an update to command and then settled down to wait.

He watched the village through the scope of his rifle. Further away, just visible on the fuzzy hills in the distance, he could see the battered old four-by-fours that had transported the goat herders to their animals and the indistinct shape of the men and their goats. Closer, within the village, the crew of the launcher had set up a canvas screen and were dozing beneath it, sheltering from the sun. He breathed slow and easy, placing each member of the crew in the middle of the reticule one after the other. Five hundred yards was nothing. He would have been able to slot one or maybe even two of them before they even knew what was going on, but it would be neater at night, and he did not want to frighten the children.

He nudged the scope away from them, observing the women as they went to and from the small river that ran through the centre of the settlement, carrying buckets of water back to their huts. He nudged it to the right, watching the five youngsters in the madrasa. They had been allowed outside to play and run off some steam. They had a yard, bordered by a low chicken-wire fence, and they were kicking a football about. Milton watched them for a while. A couple of the boys were wearing football strips, Barcelona and Manchester United, and the cheap plastic ball that they were kicking around jerked and swerved in the gentle breeze. If they knew what the scud launcher was, and the danger it represented, they did not display it in their behaviour. They were just kids having fun. The light sound of their laughter carried up to Milton on that same wind; innocent, oblivious to the chaos that was gathering on the borders of their country that would, within days, obliterate everything in its way in a mad dash to Baghdad.

Pope and the others were out of sight on the other side of the escarpment. They had raised their own small sun screen and were sheltering beneath it. Milton felt the sweat on his back, on the back of his legs, on his scalp. He felt the wooziness in his head and reached down for his jerrycan; the water was warm, but he gulped down two mouthfuls, closing his eyes to savour the sensation before replacing the cap and putting it back in the Bergen. The small amount that was left had to last him all day. He scrubbed the sweat out of his eyes with the back of his hand and stared through the scope again.

He knew the sound the instant he heard it. A low, rumbling groan, still ten miles out. He put down his rifle and grabbed his field glasses, scanning the haze where the mountains met the deep blue of the sky. The engine grew louder and he swung left and right until he saw it: a black dot that was coming in low and fast. He centred the dot in the glasses and watched it, hoping that it was something other than what he knew it to be.

The jet was a little more than a thousand feet up, running fast, and, as it neared and separated from the haze, he started to make out the details: the stubby nose; the weapons pylons on the wings bristling with missiles and the big, onion-shaped bombs; the greedy air intakes three quarters of the way down the fuselage; the wide, split fins of the tail. Milton knew exactly what it was and why it was here: an A-10 Warthog, a tank buster, sent to take out the launcher.

He fumbled for the radio, opened the channel to command and reported that he had a visual of an incoming jet, repeating that the target they had discovered was surrounded by civilians and that the jet needed to abort. There was a delay, and then static, and then, through the hiss and pop, the forward air controller told him to stand down. Milton cursed at her and opened a wide channel, identifying himself and hailing the pilot.

There was the squawk of more static and then the pilot's voice, enveloped by the sound of his engines: 'Manilla Hotel, this is POPOV35. I've got a canal that runs north/south. There's a small village, and there's a launcher under camo in the middle.'

He hadn't heard Milton or had been told to ignore him.

Forward air control responded: 'Roger that, POPOV35. Clear to engage.'

'Roger that, Manilla Hotel. POPOV35 is rolling in.'

Milton threw his rifle down and sprinted for the village.

What happened next was unclear and, in the years that had passed since then, he had dreamt it so many times and in so many different ways that it was difficult to separate the truth from his fevered imaginings of it. He was running, as fast as he could, losing his footing in the deep sand and tumbling down the slope to the desert below, his boots scrambling for purchase and his hands sinking into the sand and dust, and then he was up again and running hard. The Hog was a couple of miles away now, the engines louder even though the pilot had throttled back so that he could take his time.

Milton ran, his boots sinking into the sand, the effort of freeing them so that he could take another step making his thighs and his calves burn. Sweat poured from his face as if it were a squeezed sponge. He made the outskirts of the village and screamed out that they needed to get away, to run. An old crone who was emptying out a pot of dirty water looked at him with alarm but stayed right where she was. He ignored her, aiming for the madrasa. He was a hundred yards away and he yelled out his warning again. The Iraqis heard him, stumbling up to their feet and reaching for their rifles before they registered the noise of the jet, realised what it portended, and ran.

Milton ran past them in the opposite direction.

The children had stopped playing now. They were looking at him in confusion. Their ball rolled gently in the wind, bumping up against the side of the yard fence. One of the boys had trotted over to get it and he was closest to Milton. He was five or six.

Milton would always remember his big, brown eyes.

He screamed at them in Arabic to run.

The confusion on the boy's face would stay with him for the rest of his life.

Too late.

Much, *much* too late.

Milton looked up at the pale underbelly of the Hog as it boomed overhead, a thousand yards above; the wing pylons were empty. It had dropped its bomb three hundred yards earlier and now half a ton of high explosives fell in a neat and graceful and perfectly judged parabola that terminated at the launcher.

Milton couldn't remember what came first: the blinding flash of white light or the roar that deafened him.

The blast picked him up and tossed him twenty feet backward in the direction that he had arrived.

The scorching hot pressure wave rolled over him, and then the wave of debris: the remains of the wooden huts, shards of metal from the launcher, the storm of grit and pebbles.

He had been dropped on his back and as he opened his eyes, he thought that he must have been blinded. The swirling cloud of black fumes was parted by the wind, revealing the same perfectly clear sky overhead. Debris was still falling from the sky around him. Pieces of cloth fluttered down, soaked in blood. The mushroom cloud unfurled overhead. He could smell the explosives. He could smell burning flesh.

He rolled and pushed himself onto his knees. A wave of pain swept over him and he had to fight to prevent himself from fainting. He looked around: no launcher, no huts, no madrasa. No children. He looked away to his right, to the skidded splashes of red across the dun brown. He looked down at his chest. His shirt was bloodied. He dabbed his fingers down the centre of his sternum, further down his ribcage, to the start of his belly. He felt the rough edge of the shrapnel that had lodged just above his navel.

Milton didn't remember very much of what had happened after that. Pope said later that he and the others in the Unit had been disturbed by the approach of the Hog and had seen him running into the village. They saw the bomb detonate and had found him on the lip of a deep crater where the launcher and the madrasa had been. He was slipping in and out of consciousness. They dragged him away. The explosion had painted the sky with a column of smoke fifteen hundred feet high and they knew that if any Iraqi units were nearby they would be sent to investigate.

Pope carried him back to the Land Rover and they drove for ten miles until they found an abandoned shack, where they stopped. They radioed for emergency medivac on their way out of the village, but there had been ground-to-air activity and the rotor-heads were proceeding cautiously; they preferred to wait until darkness. None of the other men in the patrol thought Milton would make it. He was delirious and remembered nothing. Pope tended the wound as best he could. He told him afterwards that he was sure that he would bleed out, that there was nothing he could do to stop it, but he had stayed with him, pressing a compress around the shrapnel until his hands were covered in Milton's blood and, somehow, he had staunched the flow. An American army Blackhawk was sent to exfiltrate them, guided in by a tactical beacon, and it delivered Milton to the forward operating base in Saudi. He was in theatre almost as soon as the wheels touched down.

* * *

It was trite to say that Pope had saved Milton's life. He had, though; that much was unquestionable.

There had been times in the years that followed when Milton had wished that he hadn't, that he had left him to die in the smoking ruins of the village, because that would have meant that none of what followed would ever have happened.

No Group.

No Control.

No blood on his conscience.

Recently, he had started to feel different. He had found the Rooms and the Steps and he felt, for the first time in as long as he could remember, that he had hope. Not the hope of atonement, perhaps, but the chance of a little peace.

Milton thought of Pope in the basement of Shcherbatov's dacha. He was done for unless he went after him.

Milton tried to live his life by the Steps. They had saved his life, he was quite sure about that, and he believed that if he observed them faithfully, they would keep him safe.

The Eighth Step injuncted him to make a list of the people that he had harmed.

The Ninth Step required him to make amends to all of them.

He couldn't make amends to the people who he had harmed through his work for the Group: one hundred and thirty nine of them were already dead.

He chose to interpret those two Steps to mean that he should use his skills to help others. That was how he would make things right.

Tonight, as he walked through the busy streets of Hong Kong, the monsoon rains starting to fall again, he knew that he had no choice but to do whatever it took to help his friend, even if doing so would lead to his own death.

Milton was all right with that.

29

Milton grabbed a couple of hours of sleep, rose quietly at seven and worked out in the hotel gym before getting breakfast. It was just before eleven when he returned to the room. Anna was dressed and writing an email; she logged off and closed her laptop as he came inside.

'Letting the colonel know I'm still here?' Milton asked.

'Where have you been?'

'The gym,' he said. 'I like to run. It helps me focus.'

'And last night?'

'Never mind.'

'I'm afraid I do . . .'

'Are you ready to go?'

She dropped it as a lost cause and said that she was ready.

They found a taxi in the rank outside and Milton asked the driver to take them to Nathan Road. The rain had continued to fall overnight and through the early morning and, even though the temperature was much less oppressive than it would have been during the summer months, it was still warm enough to render the city's streets cloyingly humid.

The driver followed Kimberley Road and then Nathan Road; when they arrived, it was midday and the dampness seemed to wash over them. Anna was wearing a loose dress and sandals. Milton had on the suit that the Russians had bought for him, together with one of the white T-shirts. He felt the wash of sweat in the small of his back within moments. He raised the umbrella that the hotel concierge had given him and covered them both as they made their way across the pavement.

Calling the place Chungking Mansions was misleading. That made it sound grand and opulent, and it most certainly was not that. It *was* large, though: a sprawling collection of shops, takeaways, restaurants and hundreds of hostels spread over five seventeen-storey tower blocks. Five thousand people lived here, with another ten thousand coming to visit every day. There were small hostels with a couple of rooms, large dormitories with a dozen beds, to more traditionally arranged establishments with single rooms and shared bathrooms. They were cheap, occasionally cheerful, and you got what you paid for in all of them: a night's sleep, if you were lucky, and not much else besides.

It was a vast place, choked with crowds. If you were going to submerge yourself anywhere in Hong Kong, you would do it here. You could just sink into the sprawl of humanity. You could do everything you needed to do without ever having to leave.

Milton parted a way through the crowd that had gathered outside the garish entrance and went inside. It was a confusing place, crowded corridors branching off in all directions. Chinese lanterns were suspended from the ceilings and the stallholders crammed in beneath them hawked electronic goods, clothes, DVDs, mobile phones and foods for every possible ethnicity. It was a high-rise souk, rammed full of people, especially so with the rain outside. They passed petty traders, asylum seekers, itinerant workers, small-time entre-preneurs, tourists, and the unavoidable gamut of sex workers and substance abusers. Conversations merged into an inces-sant yammer so that when Anna spoke to him he had to raise his voice to answer. There was a small arcade near the door, the machines adding their own electronic babble to the cacoph-ony, a clatter of coins as a lucky punter lined up three cherries; the screech of metal as a key-cutter copied a key; the bubble and hiss of hot oil as fries were lowered into a fryer; an argu-ment between a money changer and his customer; talk radio hosts vying with shows playing western music. The air carried the odour of hundreds of damp and sweaty bodies, the tang of sweet-and-sour sauce from a fast-food joint, the heady sweet-ness of decomposing trash.

Milton pressed through the crowd, bumping against a pair of backpackers. He found his way to a uniformed guard with an elevated position, his elbows resting on the balustrade of a flight of stairs that led up to the first floor.

The Russians had provided them with the name of the hostel where they believed Beatrix had been staying. 'Do you know the Golden Guest House?' Milton asked the man.

The man shrugged.

'It's a hostel.'

The man shrugged again, the corner of his mouth curling up in a suggestive smile.

'Here,' Anna said, pressing a ten-dollar note into his hand.

He folded the note once, then twice, and slipped it into the breast pocket of his shirt. 'Other side of building,' he said. He gave them directions and left them to find it.

30

The hostel was on the third floor at the end of a maze of windowless corridors that Milton found intensely claustrophobic. He had completely lost his sense of direction and, the deeper they penetrated the warren of rooms, the more vulnerable he felt. An ambush here would be difficult to escape.

The Golden Guest House was announced by a painted sign and the open door beneath gave onto a tiny lobby with a bored-looking man behind the desk. It was hot and sticky. A broken desk fan sat impotently on a low table between two battered sofas, yellowed stuffing leaking out between rents in the leather that looked like they had been torn open at the point of a knife.

The man behind the desk was small and sallow-faced, eating a piece of greasy chicken with his fingers as he watched American wrestling. He barely looked up as Milton and Anna entered.

'I'm looking for a woman,' Milton said.

'We all look for woman,' the man replied with a lewd smirk at Anna.

'A friend of mine. I think she's staying here.'

'Can't talk about guest. Confidential.'

Milton had a photograph of Beatrix that the Russians had provided. It was old, from before the time of the hit on Shcherbatov, and she was dressed in what Milton thought was a police uniform. The likeness was good from what he could remember, but it was years out of date; time would have aged her, surely, not to mention the changes she would have effected herself. He laid it flat on the counter and left a hundred-dollar bill on top of it.

The clerk sucked the grease from his fingers and then wiped them on his shirt, pocketed the bill and turned the photograph around so that he could look at it properly. He put a finger up his nostril and turned it around absently. 'I don't know. Maybe I know her, maybe I don't. Hard to be sure.'

Milton dropped another hundred on the counter and, as the man reached for it, Milton caught his hand and squeezed.

'Ow!' he said. 'That hurts!'

'You take me to her room now, all right?'

Milton knew pressure points. His thumb was pushing on the nerve, sending exquisite bolts of pain up the arm.

The man winced and thought better of trying to inveigle another hundred out of him. 'Okay, I show.'

Milton smiled politely and released the man's hand.

He led them through a narrow corridor to a tiny box of a room with a single bed, a suitcase propped against the wall and an old-fashioned cathode-ray portable television set resting atop a rickety dresser. The A/C unit above the bed expectorated a trail of moisture that had stained the wall. There were no windows and, although there was a bathroom, it was only just big enough for the toilet, with the result that the shower head was directly overhead.

'How long has she been here?' Milton asked.

'Don't know. Six month, seven month, maybe more.'

'On her own?'

'Yes.'

'Have you spoken to her?'

'No. No speak with guests.'

'And where is she now?'

He found a little courage. 'Who are you?'

'Friends,' Milton said patiently. 'We need to find her. Where is she?'

The man hesitated, calculating how much he stood to lose if his guest left in disgust at his impropriety against the damage this intimidating westerner might cause. He dipped his head and whispered, 'She eats here, in Chungking.'

'Where?'

'There is a place. Syed Bukhara. Malaysian. Floor Seven, Block E.'

*   *   *

It took them another hour to find their way to the restaurant. There were dozens of places, mostly very small, and although Syed Bukhara was a little bigger than the average, it was still only big enough for a half-dozen plastic picnic tables and matching chairs. There was a Formica countertop, a revolving display case that advertised sickly-looking desserts and an

Indian man in a turban who showed them to the only empty table. The overhead lights were bright and harsh and the laminated menu was stained with fragments of rice and sauce that seemed to have been welded to it. Milton scanned it. The prices were cheap. His appetite was aroused by the aroma that was coming from the kitchen.

Milton ordered Nasi Lemak with egg – a Malaysian comfort food that he remembered from a particularly messy assignment in Kuala Lumpur. Anna ordered the mutton Bukhara biryani special. The dishes arrived and what they lacked in presentation they made up for in taste. Anna couldn't finish hers and so Milton helped, polishing off the meat and basmati rice. By the time he was finished, he was sated. They ordered two cups of Indian chai tea and drank them slowly. When they had finished those, they ordered a couple more.

Milton's chair was facing the corridor. He made sure that it was angled so that he wouldn't be too easy to spot. He didn't think that Beatrix would run, but he didn't want to take the chance.

They had been there for two hours when Milton finally gave up.

'If she comes in here, she's not coming today.'

'We'll come back later?'

'Tomorrow,' Milton said.

'What now?'

'I need a shower.'

31

Milton had no interest in waiting in their hotel room. The rains cleared away in the afternoon and he decided to go out for a run.

'Where are you going?' she asked.

'Out,' he said. 'I need some exercise. I'll be back this evening.'

'What exercise?'

'A run. Is that all right?'

Anna stood, too, and slipped her feet into her sandals. 'Do you mind if I come?'

He paused at the door. 'I don't know, Anna. I'm not feeling particularly sociable.'

'It's not to keep an eye on you,' she qualified. 'I don't want to stay here all afternoon.'

'Then don't. Go out.'

Milton looked at her. He felt the same primal response again, quickly suppressing it, and relented.

'Fine,' he said. 'We'll need some kit.'

He opened the door and they made their way to the lobby. Anna smiled sweetly at him as they waited for the lift to arrive. Perhaps it would be useful to have her around. He didn't know very much about her, and that was remiss of him; anything at all could prove to be useful. And, perhaps, she could be persuaded, or tricked, into passing him a little information about Shcherbatov and his plans for Control and Pope.

*   *   *

There was a small sports shop not too far from the hotel and they visited it to buy running shoes and socks, vests and shorts. They returned to the hotel, changed in the gym and then went back onto the street. Milton had run around Hong Kong before; the pavements themselves were not suitable, too clogged with people and sometimes too steep, plus the air was often thick with smog that could make for an unpleasant experience. He had learned his lesson and researched alternative routes. As they headed out, he decided to run his favourite of them.

They headed south-west through the Zoological and Botanical Gardens, past the Ladies' Recreation Club and then started to ascend the Peak. A gentle breeze blowing in off the bay took a little of the edge off the humidity. It was still hot, though, and it didn't take long for Milton to work up a sweat. Anna kept the pace beside him. She was fit and strong and it was obvious that she ran often. The climb up Old Peak Road grew steeper and steeper and, eventually, she started to flag. Milton dropped his pace and she reeled him back in again.

They reached Peak Tower and ran around Lugard Road. It was car-free and, as a result, it was busy with dog walkers, other runners and families. There was a tower at the top, an upside-down wok-shaped building with a galleria that contained shops and restaurants. The route was mostly shaded and, as they got up high, it offered postcard views over Central and Wanchai. They paused at the ten-kilometre mark to look out at the vista: the sparkling skyscrapers and the deep blue of Victoria Harbour all the way to the green hills of the New Territories, the panorama slowly melting into the pink and orange of early twilight.

He was a little short of breath, but Anna was breathing harder.

'All right to keep going?'

'Sure.'

'Mostly downhill from here.'

He led the way again as they wound back around the Peak, picking up Harlech Road on the backside until they were at the Peak Tower again. They followed Findlay Road until it met Severn Road, home to the most expensive property in the world. That was the turn-off point, and they ran back down into Central and made their way towards the hotel. It was a fifteen-kilometre route, all told, and Milton's muscles were tingling as they finally stopped to warm down.

There was a small pharmacy across the road.

'Want a bottle of water?' he said.

'Sure.'

'Hold on.'

Milton went inside, picked up two half-litre bottles and took them to the desk. He paid for them and spoke to the pharmacist for a moment. Temazepam should not have been available without a prescription, but he explained that he had been unable to sleep properly all week and that he needed it badly. A twenty-dollar note laid on the counter was sufficient incentive and, with a nod of understanding, the man disappeared into the back and came back with a box of Restoril. Milton thanked him and went back outside to join Anna again.

32

They went back to the hotel to shower and when Anna disappeared down to the lobby – to file a report, Milton guessed – he spent a couple of hours with his book. When she returned, he suggested that they go out to dinner. She smiled brightly at the suggestion; it was an innocent happiness that must have been inspired, he supposed, by the thought that she had finally broken through the hard carapace that he sheltered behind. It almost made him feel bad to see it. He knew then that he would be able to do what he needed to do.

She suggested that he choose where they eat and he picked Caprice, a favourite of his from years ago. They took a taxi and it was nearly eight when they arrived.

There was something very modern about the place, and yet something proper and solid. The lobby was crafted between two floor-to-ceiling displays of wine bottles – with some enviable vintages on show – and the maître d' led them through a dining room that was encased with dark wood panelling and equipped with luxurious leather sofas and armchairs. The kitchen was open and situated in the middle of the dining area, with nothing to separate the diners from the delicious smells that were created or the quiet, determined communication between the chefs.

The room was busy, with local Hong Kong Chinese and expat diners enjoying their meals, filling the space with engaged conversation and the sound of expensive cutlery on expensive plates. Milton followed in Anna's wake and watched the heads of the other diners turn to look at her. Her summer dress was creased and marked and her face was streaked with sweat and dust and yet she was still extraordinary to look at.

All of the tables enjoyed a view of Victoria Harbour, and theirs was especially good. Milton looked out over the broad curve of the harbour. Lights were strung between the trees in the garden and then, out on the water, colourful junks rose and fell on the shallow swells.

They perused the elaborate, leather-bound menus. Milton beckoned to the sommelier and turned to his companion.

'What will you have?' he asked.

'Do you have a recommendation?'

'Not really,' he said. 'I don't drink.'

'Not at all?'

'No.'

'Why not?'

'I used to drink too much,' he said simply. 'So I stopped.'

'Do you mind if I . . .'

He waved it off. 'No, of course not. Have whatever you like.'

She replaced the wine list face down on the table and turned to the sommelier. 'I would like a gin and tonic, please. Hendrick's. Fill the glass with ice, all the way to the top, and a slice of cucumber.' She returned to her study of the menu as the sommelier left. 'Do you know what you want?' she asked. 'Please, don't be frugal. The Kremlin is paying.' She smiled at her own joke, trying to encourage him, too, but it fell rather flat; it dragged Milton away from the potential pleasure of a meal in her company and back to the reality of why they were here together.

Milton summoned the waiter.

The man arrived and addressed Anna. 'Madam?'

'The langoustine lasagne and then the wagyu striploin, please.'

The waiter turned to Milton. 'And sir?'

'The vegetable panache, please, and then suckling pig rack.'

The man complimented them on their choices and left the table.

'You must forgive me,' Anna said. 'I am very particular about what I eat and drink. It comes from my background. There was very little luxury when I was a child. Times were difficult. And now, when I'm working, it's usually on my own. It makes things more bearable if you can go to nice restaurants and know a little about what's on the menu.'

'You were born in Russia?'

'Volgograd,' she said. 'Have you been there?'

'Never.'

'I wouldn't bother. It is not a pleasant place. My father worked for the KGB. We moved around a lot, depending on where he was posted. We spent time in Kenya, Somalia, Vietnam. I was a bit of an embassy brat.'

'Any brothers or sisters?'

'Just me.'

'Where did you study?'

'Moscow. We moved back when I was sixteen. The People's Friendship University of Russia. Master's degree in economics. I could have had a job with a Russian bank, made a lot of money perhaps, but I was recruited by my tutor as soon as I graduated. They had different plans for me, I suppose. My father was proud. It wasn't something I was able to turn down. I moved to London and worked for a couple of banks. And I met my husband there.'

'You're married?' he said. He pointed to her naked hand. 'You don't . . .'

'Divorced. He was American. It was for the passport.'

She reported it completely matter-of-factly, as if getting married was something that had needed to be checked off a list.

'How long were you there for?'

'In London? I stayed for a few years.'

'And after that?'

'New York, originally. I worked in international real estate.'

'That was the cover?'

'Of course. There was no business. There never was. It was a fantasy. Just a desk. It was a useful front and a good way to pass funds to me.'

'What were you doing there?'

She smiled and shook her head. 'No, Captain Milton, that wouldn't do. Some things will have to remain secret. You understand, I'm sure.'

'All right. So why don't you tell me why were you in Texas?'

'That was for you. I was given instructions that an asset was thought to be in the area. We didn't know where, exactly, so several of us were moved to the south to wait.'

'Several? There are more of you?'

She smiled. 'Many more. The CIA has been focused on external threats for too long. It is easy to work in America if you know what you are doing.'

'So you just upped and left? Do you live alone?'

She smiled mischievously. 'Do I have a boyfriend, you mean?'

He knew that the conversation was pulling him in the direction she wanted, but he didn't feel like resisting her any more. 'Do you?'

'There was someone, but it was for work. I doubt I'll see him again.'

Milton left a pause and then allowed her a smile. 'A little better,' he remarked.

'How do you mean?'

'I like to know the person I'm having dinner with,' he said. 'I think I'm getting there.'

He raised his glass.

She touched hers to his. '*Nasdrovje*,' she said.

'Cheers.'

The waiter arrived with the lasagne and the panache and they ate for a time in silence. The food was as delicious as Milton remembered.

'Do you mind if I ask you something?' she said.

'Depends what it is.'

'Some things will have to remain secret?' Her eyes gleamed.

He smiled. 'Something like that.'

'You had a bad dream on the flight . . .'

'I told you,' he said sharply. 'It was just a bad pill.'

Her eyes clouded with concern.

'I'm sorry,' she said. 'You don't have to answer.'

'It's all right.' He gazed out into the darkness of the bay. 'It's something I saw a long time ago. It's not a very good memory. Occasionally I dream about it.'

They were quiet again as they finished their starters. Milton watched Anna's face: she looked deep in thought as if, he thought, she was trying out conversational lines to be sure that she didn't spoil the mood.

She finished the lasagne, placed the cutlery on the plate and looked up, a bright smile on her face. 'You know,' she said, 'I was pleased that they asked me to go and get you in Texas. It was something of a coup. You are famous with Russian intelligence. Well, not you personally' – she corrected herself quickly, although he knew that she had meant him – 'your Group. Group Fifteen. You are famous and feared.'

'I'm not a member of the Group any more.'

'Nevertheless . . .'

He frowned and, when he spoke, it was quietly. 'It's nothing to be proud of. What we did. What *I* did. I have a lot of blood on my hands, Anna. Some of them probably deserved what they got. The others, I don't know. Maybe not.' He felt awkward talking about it; it made the prospect of a drink more difficult to ignore. He remembered the meeting and the sense of calmness he had felt. He needed to change the subject. 'How did you like the lasagne?'

'It was delicious. I've had a good day and now I'm having a lovely evening. It's just a pity . . .'

'What is?'

'You know. The circumstances. Now. The job.' She stopped, warned by a blank look on Milton's face.

'That's just the way it is,' he said. 'Orders. You're doing what you've been told to do.'

He paused and turned his head to the window again. The conversation was becoming more intimate than was appropriate. There were some subjects that Milton would not discuss, with anyone, and she had an open and inviting manner that made it easy to forget his boundaries. He had already said too much. He chided himself: she was a Russian agent. He was only here – in Hong Kong, having dinner with her – because they had a gun to his head. A man he owed a blood debt to had been arrested, beaten and was being held God knows where, having God knows what done to him. That was the only reason Milton was here. Pope was the only reason that he hadn't already abandoned her, blended in with the multitude and disappeared from view again.

He was having dinner with her under sufferance and not through choice. Unfortunately, however many times he told himself that, he knew it wasn't really true.

33

The rest of the meal went well. The food was excellent and the conversation was good. Anna loosened up even more after her gin and then she ordered a couple of glasses of wine with her main course. She became a little more indiscreet about her work, although Milton was sure that some of it was calculated; passing on a little harmless gossip here and there in an attempt to inveigle herself into his own confidences.

She excused herself between the main course and dessert and Milton took his chance. He had prepared earlier, before they left for dinner: he had popped three of the temazepam tablets from their blister pack, ground them together and swept the fine powder into a folded triangle of paper. Now, he reached across the table for her unfinished glass of wine and, after checking that he wasn't observed, tipped the powder into it. It dissolved quickly and without any sign of residue.

Anna returned to the table and asked him to talk about his background. Assuming that she knew it all anyway, he did. He told her about the peripatetic early years spent following his father's career around the oil states in the Gulf, his parents' death, the largely unsuccessful time at private school and then his years reading law at Cambridge. He explained how he had eschewed the career at the bar that had seemed mapped out for him and how he had joined the Green Jackets instead. There was his first posting in Gibraltar, the time spent in the Gulf for the first Iraq war and then the Provinces. Talking about that brought him right back to Pope again and, not wishing to dwell on that tonight, he had been glad that their desserts were finished and cleared away and Anna proposed that they return to the hotel.

Anna summoned the waiter, asked for the bill, paid it in cash and left a large tip on the table. She rose, suddenly a little unsteadily.

'I'm afraid I'm a little drunk,' she said.

'Here.' Milton offered her his arm and, with her clinging onto it, he led the way out of the restaurant and onto the street outside.

It had started to rain again; gently at first, a fine gossamer mist that dampened the face, but then, as they stood waiting to flag a taxi, it fell harder and harder until it was drumming thunderously on the awning above them.

Milton took out a packet of cigarettes and offered Anna one. She took it, ducking her head to accept his light and exposing the nape of her long, white neck.

'How are you feeling?' he asked.

'A little . . . fuzzy. I . . . I . . .' She stammered for the words and, slowly, a frown that might have been realisation broke across her face. 'You . . . you . . .' she started again, but the words fluttered away, the thought incomplete and unexpressed.

A taxi pulled up. She was asleep on his shoulder before it had even pulled away.

34

Milton awoke and reached out for his watch on the bedside table. He scrubbed the sleep from his eyes and checked the time: it was nine the next morning.

He let his head fall back on the pillow and closed his eyes again. He was tempted to go back to sleep, but it was already later than he had intended and he had plenty to do. Anna was still in her bed, and he got out of bed slowly and deliberately, careful not to wake her. She was lying on her front, the sheets pulled halfway down her back. Milton had laid her there, still dressed. Her breathing was deep and very relaxed. He wasn't sure how long the effect of the temazepam would last, but he figured that he had a little while yet. She would be able to guess where he had gone, but he would have a head start, at least. He hoped that he could find Beatrix Rose before she could get there.

He went into the bathroom, dressed and then quietly left the room.

Milton took a taxi to Chungking Mansion and made his way to Syed Bukhara again. It was ten when he took a seat at the same table in the restaurant as before and started what he suspected would be the first in a series of cups of tea.

* * *

He didn't have long to wait.

'Hello, Milton.'

He turned: there was a woman behind him, and, for a moment, he didn't recognise her. It was eight years, that was true, but even so. She was thin, the structure of her bones easily visible through a face that had far less shape than Milton remembered. Her skin looked brittle and dry, like parchment, and her eyes, which had once been bright and full of fire, were dull and lifeless, obscured by a film of rheum. She looked ill.

'Number One,' he said.

She shook her head. 'Not any more. And not for a long time.'

There was a wariness in her face as she regarded the few other diners in the restaurant. She moved gingerly, as if it gave her pain, and, as she came around the table and passed directly in front of him, Milton saw with dismay that the emaciation in her face was symptomatic of a more general malaise; she had been beautifully curvaceous before, but that was all gone now. She was wearing a flimsy blouse with short sleeves and as she braced her arms on the table to lower herself down into the seat, he could see the bony protuberances of her elbows and the shape of the bones in her wrists. She moved with deliberate care. It was as if she had aged thirty years in the space of ten.

She had a bag with her and, as she sat down, she arranged it in her lap and slid a hand inside.

'I've got a gun,' she said. 'It's aimed right at your balls. Ten seconds, Milton. What the fuck are you doing here?'

Point blank. She wouldn't miss.

'I could ask you the same thing.'

'Five seconds.'

'I want to talk to you.'

'Did Control send you?'

'No,' he said.

'I don't believe you.'

'This has nothing to do with him. Or the Group. You have my word.'

'Better make me believe that, Milton. I'd rather not shoot you.'

Milton was calm. 'Control doesn't know where I am,' he said. 'He doesn't know where you are, either. If he did, we wouldn't be having this conversation, would we? I would already have shot you.'

She chuckled mirthlessly. 'No, Milton, you wouldn't. I've been following you since you came here to look for me yesterday. I'm disappointed. I taught you to be observant and I'm very out of practice. Go on, why are you here?'

'I'm here of my own accord. I'm out of the Group. I quit. I told Control a while ago. Can't say he took too kindly to the idea. He's already tried to kill me twice.'

'Keep going.'

Milton didn't demur. He told her everything that had happened. He started at the beginning, all the way back to what had happened in London after his last assignment in the Alps, because he knew she would need to have the context to understand what had happened next. He told her about his argument with Control.

'So you resigned,' she said.

'I tried. It wasn't accepted.'

'You know you can't . . .'

'Yes,' he interrupted. 'So he kept telling me.'

He explained about the attempt to murder him in London that had very nearly been successful, how he had been shot by Callan and how he had fled to South America. He told her about Ciudad Juárez, and Control's second attempt to bring him back in, and about how he had escaped and fled to San Francisco.

'So you're a wanted man?'

'Looks that way, doesn't it?'

'Control isn't the sort of person you'd want chasing you.'

'He certainly is relentless,' he said with a wry smile. 'Is that enough for you?'

She withdrew her hand from the bag. 'For the time being.'

'So what about you?'

Her posture stiffened. 'What about me?'

'Why are you here?'

'It's a long story.'

The waiter looked over at her with a friendly, knowing smile. 'The usual, miss?'

'Please.'

She put her hand back into her bag and, for a moment, Milton thought she was going for the gun again. She rummaged for a moment, unable to find whatever it is she wanted.

'Cigarette?' Milton offered.

'You still smoke?'

'Tried to stop,' he said.

'It'll kill you.'

'So will lots of things. I decided I might as well have one vice. They let you smoke in here?'

She looked at him with mild amusement. 'Seriously, Milton? Look around. You can do whatever you want.'

He took the unfinished packet from his pocket and offered it to her.

She took it and held it up. 'Winston's?'

'Afraid so. They're not great.'

'You want to tell me why you've got a packet of Russian cigarettes?'

'I was in Moscow. That's why I'm here.'

She took two, leaving one on the table. Milton took out his oxidised Ronson lighter, thumbed the flame and held it out for her. She dipped her head to it, the blouse falling open at the neck and revealing the angular points of her clavicle. Milton took one for himself and left the packet on the table.

She leaned back and inhaled hungrily. 'So who's the pretty girl?'

'Her name is Anna Vasil'yevna Kushchyenko.'

'Where is she?'

181

'At the hotel.'

'She looked unwell last night.'

'You were at the restaurant?'

'Outside. What's wrong with her?'

'I drugged her.'

'How chivalrous.'

'I wanted to see you on my own.'

'What is she? Russian intelligence?'

'SVR,' Milton said.

She drew down on her cigarette. 'So what does a pretty Russian intelligence agent have to do with you?'

He leant back in the chair and drew on his cigarette. 'She was sent to recruit me.'

Beatrix cocked an eyebrow at that. 'For what?'

The waiter returned with two cups of Indian chai tea. She thanked him and waited until he had returned to the counter before she spoke again.

'To recruit you for what, Milton?'

'They wanted me to find you.'

She shook her head sharply. 'Whatever it is, I'm not interested.'

'Just hear me out.'

'Do you think I'd be somewhere like this if I wanted to be found?'

'Just let me give you a little bit of background first. I've come halfway around the world to find you. Humour me.'

She settled back in the chair and fixed him with a steady glare. She moved her hand close to the mouth of the bag again. 'Give me another fag.'

He did as she asked.

'You've got five minutes and then I'm gone.'

'Do you remember my first assignment?' Milton asked.

Her eyes narrowed just a little. 'Of course I remember it. It was a disaster.'

'You remember the two targets?'

'Yes,' she said carefully.

'DOLLAR and SNOW. We never knew anything about them.'

'What's your point, Milton? We never knew anything about any of them. They're just names.'

'DOLLAR was Anastasia Ivanovna Semenko and SNOW was Pascha Shcherbatov. They were both Russian agents. Turns out Shcherbatov is a colonel in the SVR now.'

'Where are you going with this? It doesn't matter that they were spooks. I killed my fair share. You would have, too.'

'I know. That's not the point. Semenko and Shcherbatov weren't targeted because they were spooks. They were sent to London because the Russians had a tip-off that Control could be bought. They had assets inside the Iraqi government who said he was introducing arms dealers to the right people. So Semenko set herself up as a dealer, said she wanted an in with the Syrians. Control said he could arrange that for her – for the right price. They had him. Photographs, financial records, everything they needed. They were going to flip him or they were going to burn him. He'd proposed a meeting to talk it over. They were going to see him when we hit them. He set the whole thing up. The whole operation was all about him trying to save his own neck.'

She listened intently, her brow occasionally furrowing, chain-smoking her way through another two cigarettes. 'How do you know this?'

Milton told her about his trip to Russia to meet Shcherbatov and the story he had told him in the dacha. She didn't look surprised by any of it.

'And what does this have to do with you?'

'Shcherbatov wanted me to find you.'

'But why would you do anything for him?'

'There's another agent. Michael Pope. You won't know him, he joined after you disappeared.'

'No, I do remember him,' she said. 'Tall, dark hair? We looked at him before we chose you,' she explained, punctuating the words with an absent stab of the cigarette.

'He was made Number One after I got out.'

'How did he end up in Russia?'

'There was a job in the south of France. Control sent him after Shcherbatov again. He got caught. If I don't help him, he doesn't have much of a future.'

She waved that away. 'Those are the breaks,' she said. 'He would have known the risks.'

'True,' Milton said, 'but he saved my life once. And I can't leave him there.'

She knocked a long ash into the empty teacup. 'You haven't explained what any of this has to do with me.'

'Shcherbatov thinks you took evidence from the car.'

She shrugged. 'So?'

'Did you?'

'No,' she said dismissively, although he saw the flinch before she spoke.

'Beatrix?' he pressed. 'Did you?'

'I said no,' she said sharply, although he registered the movement in her eyes and he knew that she was lying. 'I can't help you, Milton.'

'And I can't leave Pope to rot in a gulag.'

'That's very valiant, but there's nothing I can do. I'm sorry.'

'I need your help. Please, Beatrix.' The respect between them was old, frozen by the passage of time, but he hoped there was enough of it left for her to consider helping him. 'Pope needs you.'

'I can't.'

'I think you need me, too.'

Now her eyes flashed with sudden anger. 'Why would you say something stupid like that?'

'Beatrix,' he said carefully, remembering her temper. 'Look at where you are. Look at yourself.'

'Fuck off, Milton.'

She waved an impatient arm at him and the motion caused her sleeve to ride a little up her arm, revealing the lower part of a cursive tattoo that he remembered. The fragment said '—ABELLA' and Milton remembered seeing it before, and asking what it meant.

He took a breath and thought about what he was going to say. He knew it would be inflammatory, but he didn't have any other cards left to play.

'The tattoo,' he said, pointing, 'on your arm. You told me that was for your daughter, Isabella. Do you remember?'

She stood.

'What happened to her? Where is she?'

'We're finished,' Beatrix said. 'Don't try to find me again. I don't want to be found. Do you understand?'

She stalked away from the table without a backward glance.

35

Milton stayed at the table for thirty minutes, smoking a couple of cigarettes and worrying about the content of their conversation and how weak and ill Beatrix had looked, and how little he had achieved.

He was about to settle the bill when Anna arrived. Her eyes flashed with fury; with him, and, he guessed, with herself. He had played her very well yesterday, persuading her that he was warming to her to lower her guard just enough that he could put her out of the way for a few hours. He had brought it to an expert conclusion at dinner. He knew that she would feel embarrassed; she had offered herself to him and he had not only rejected the offer, he had turned the tables completely and used the *detente* between them as a means to incapacitate her. She was a beautiful girl; he doubted that she was used to being treated like that. There might have been some consolation for her if he had admitted that he found her almost irresistibly attractive, but he did not. He guessed, from the steeliness in her eyes, that she would have hit him. He would have deserved it, too.

'You're going to have to get over it,' he told her. 'It was necessary. She would never have come out if we were here together.'

'What? You met her?'

'Yes,' he said. 'Forty minutes ago.'

The anger drained out of her. 'And? Will she help?'

'No.'

'What do you mean, no?'

'I mean, no. She's not in the best shape, Anna.'

'That's not good enough, Milton. You can't give up.'

'Who said I was giving up?'

'Where is she?'

'I can guess,' he said. 'I'm going to go and see her now.'

'I'm coming too.'

'No,' he said. 'You're not.'

'You're forgetting—'

'She's been hiding here for the best part of a decade, Anna. She's paranoid. And you should remember what she used to do before she came here. How do you think she'll react if she thinks Russian intelligence have started to follow her? No, don't answer, I'll tell you; she'll shoot you, and then she'll likely shoot me.'

She started to protest again and he held up a hand to forestall her.

'I'll go and speak to her again. I think I can persuade her, but you are going to have to trust me.'

'After what you did?'

'Even after that. If I can get her to co-operate, then you can meet her. That's the only way this is going to work, Anna.'

* * *

Milton didn't need to follow Beatrix; he knew where she was going. He got lost amid the commotion as soon as he reached the ground floor and only found the familiar corridor an hour later. The same man was behind the desk, an illegal feed of Premiership football on the television. Milton gave him another hundred dollars and went through into the corridor that led to the rooms.

Beatrix was lying on the bed, breathing almost without sound. She was covered with a single sheet, the shape of her gaunt body visible beneath. The room was smoky and smelled sickly bittersweet. There was a joint in an ashtray, and it sent languid smoke drifting up to the ceiling. She was deep in sleep and yet she did not looked relaxed; her face was troubled and, as he watched, the muscles in her cheek started to twitch, the sudden jerk reflected and amplified by an unconscious spasm in her right leg. The air-conditioning unit coughed and spluttered, gobbets of water falling from it and splashing against the wall and floor. The door was open, and cold, harsh light from the lobby leaked inside.

Milton stepped all the way inside; the room was so small that he had to squeeze right up against the bed before he was able to close the door. He knelt down. There was an ivory pipe on the bed next to Beatrix's head: the long bamboo stem was decorated with Chinese inscriptions along its length and it was fitted with a blue and white porcelain bowl. Milton picked up the pipe; the bowl was detachable and, as he unscrewed it, he saw a congealed brown paste gathered inside. There was a wooden tray on the bed next to her knees complete with a funnel-shaped lamp made of nickel silver, a spare pipe and two extra pipe bowls. A small folded paper envelope was on the tray. Milton picked it up and opened it. There was half a gram of brown powder inside with the consistency of ground cinnamon. His stomach plunged. He had been to the East more than enough times to recognise opium.

Now he knew why Beatrix looked as bad as she did.

He knew why she had chosen to live in a place like this: you could find anything you wanted in Chungking Mansion, legal or not. Finding someone with opium to sell would be a simple matter indeed.

Milton took the tray from the bed and placed it quietly on the floor.

He let her sleep. It was another three hours before she finally woke. She stirred, turning over so that she was facing him, and her shallow breathing altered a little. He saw her eyes open, staring right at him.

'Bella?' she said in a quiet voice, and then she closed her eyes again.

She woke properly twenty minutes later. She opened her eyes wide and gave a shudder.

'Beatrix,' Milton whispered. He put his right hand on her shoulder.

Her breathing accelerated and her right hand flailed, searching for something. It stabbed under the pillow and, when it emerged, it was holding a small pistol.

Milton reached down and caught her wrist in his hand. She was weak and he pressed her arm gently down against the mattress. 'It's me, Beatrix. It's John.'

Her whisper was so quiet that he had to strain his ears to catch the words. 'I told you,' she said. 'I can't help you.'

'That's fine,' he replied, his hand still on her wrist. 'I won't ask again. I'm here for you now. I want to help *you*.'

She laughed, weak and bitter, the noise tearing into a ragged cough. 'You can't.'

'Tell me what's happened.'

'Leave me alone, Milton. It's pointless. You can't do anything.'

'Just tell me. Maybe I can.'

She shook her head and was silent for a moment. Milton thought that she had gone back to sleep again when she gulped and he realised that she was crying silent tears.

'Beatrix, where's Isabella?'

36

Beatrix gradually regained her strength and when she did, Milton helped her to stand so that she could go over to the cupboard.

She was naked apart from her underwear, but she was too vacant to be shy. She had lost so much weight that her ribs showed clearly and, as she turned and bent down to pull up her jeans, he could see the individual vertebrae in her back. He saw the tattoo with Isabella on her right arm and, as she turned, he saw more ink: eight bars of solid black, one after the other, running down from underneath her arm towards her waist. She opened the door, picked out a clean T-shirt and put it on.

'You got any more smokes?'

He took out the packet and gave it to her. 'Keep it.'

'I just want one.' She fingered one from the carton and lit it.

The atmosphere in the room was still heady and Milton felt the beginnings of a headache. 'What do you say we get some air?'

She shrugged limply. 'I don't care.'

She put on a jacket and allowed him to lead the way down to Nathan Road.

'There's a bar I know around the corner,' she suggested.

'I don't do bars. Somewhere else?'

'You don't want a drink?' she asked. 'I want a drink.'

'It's not that I don't want one … it's just that … well, I don't.'

'At all?'

He nodded ruefully. 'You're looking at a new man,' he said.

'You were a soldier, Milton. I've never met a soldier who doesn't drink.'

'Long story,' he replied. 'I'll tell you later.' They were passing a coffee shop. 'How about here?'

She shrugged and they went inside.

Milton ordered two strong coffees and two apple doughnuts. Beatrix had found a table at the back of the room and had taken the seat that was facing out, into the street. She was extremely careful, Milton thought. Old habits died hard. He took the coffees and the doughnuts over and sat down opposite her.

'Get this down you,' he said, sliding the plate across the table.

She picked it up and took a big bite.

'What's going on?' Milton asked.

Beatrix stopped for a moment, as if hesitating at a crossroads, considering each possible choice and the consequences that might flow from it. Milton waited, listening to the sound of cutlery ringing against crockery, the low buzz of conversation and the electric hum of the city outside.

'What Shcherbatov told you. About the operation. It's true.'

'How do you know that?'

'There was a briefcase in the car after we hit it. It was just habitual. I saw it, I took it. I went back home before we debriefed and I opened it there. Those things you said: the photographs, the flash drives. They were in the case.'

'Did you look at them?'

'Just the photographs. They were enough for me to know something was wrong. Control hasn't been a field agent for *years*, Milton. In all the time I worked for him, the only time I saw him away from his desk was for that job. I'd certainly never seen him meeting a target before. That didn't make any sense at all. I knew that something was wrong.'

'What did you do?'

'I copied the flash drives and hid them and then I went in with the photographs. I asked him to explain them. He couldn't, of course. He tried, but it was all bullshit. I was about ready to quit before that assignment, like you, and that was just the final straw as far as I was concerned. I played along with him, gave him the answers that he wanted to hear, and then I went home.'

She paused and swallowed, her skinny neck bulging once and then twice.

Milton pressed gently. 'What happened?'

'He'd sent five agents. They were waiting for me. They had my husband and daughter. They had a gun on my little girl.'

She looked down, her eyes closing. She stayed like that for twenty seconds, her chest rising and falling with each deep lungful of breath that she took. When she looked up again, her eyes glistened with tears.

'I knew if I didn't do something they'd kill all three of us, so I waited for my chance and went for them. My husband was shot, I got a round in the shoulder, but I managed to fuck one of them up pretty good. If she wasn't dead she'd be smoking these,' she held up the cigarette, 'through the hole I put in her throat. The other one got my daughter.'

'Got?'

'Grabbed her. They—' The words choked in her throat. She stood up and went to the counter for more cigarettes. Milton remained at the table, staring at the half-eaten doughnut, unsure quite what to say.

Beatrix returned, tossing the cigarettes onto the table. There was fresh steel in her face.

Milton started, 'You don't have to say . . .'

'It was a stalemate,' she said over him. 'I had a gun on them, they had her. What was I going to do?' She tore off the cellophane wrapper, opened the carton and took out a cigarette. Milton lit it for her. 'The only thing I could do was run. I got on the Eurostar, went through the tunnel and then kept going. Got on a plane in Barcelona and came here. It seemed as good a place as any to stop. Been here ever since.'

'Where is she now?' Milton asked. 'Your daughter?'

'I don't know,' she said. 'They emailed a picture a week after it all happened.' She took a slim wallet from her jeans pocket, opened it and took out a photograph. She laid it on the table and Milton took it. The girl had a happy, open face, a ready smile and a cascade of curls that gathered on her shoulders. The picture had been taken in an anonymous room, the little girl sitting in front of a large TV with beige walls in the background. She was playing with a doll. 'She looks fine, but I know that was a reminder. A warning. Control will have her in care somewhere. She'll be alive. He knows that as long as he has her, that's the one thing that'll stop me coming back and tearing his throat out.'

'The tattoos on your ribs,' Milton said, pointing to his own trunk. 'That's one for every year, right?'

'That's right. Eight years.'

'But you can't stay here.'

'Why not?'

He leant forward and spoke urgently, 'Because I found you. Shcherbatov knows where you are. If I can't persuade you to help them, he's not going to give up. He wants what you have about Control. He'll just send someone else who won't ask as nicely.'

'You didn't find me, Milton, *I* found *you*. And that threat doesn't work if you've got nothing left to lose.'

He pressed ahead. 'What about Control?'

'What about him?'

'If he finds out where you are, you know what will happen. He's still there. He hasn't stopped.'

'Look at me, Milton. You're not listening. Do you think any of that frightens me? Shcherbatov? Control?' She shaped her fingers into the shape of a gun and pressed the tips against her temple. 'You think the gun's for defence? You know how many times I've wanted to put a bullet in my head and lost my nerve? Every day.'

197

Milton felt his stomach turn and he reached across and took her wrist; there was no resistance in her arm as he gently lowered it and held it against the table.

'I can't even do that. I'm fucked up. They come over here and do it for me, I'm telling you, they'd be doing me a fucking favour.' She sucked down on the smoke and gazed out into the street. 'My life is over. My husband is dead. I lost my daughter. I've got no money. I'm a drug addict. I'm done, Milton. Finished. How do you think this is going to end?'

'There must be something you can do.'

'You got any ideas? I'm all ears.'

'Something, anything. It would have been better than coming here to all . . . this.'

'This?'

'The opium, for a start.'

'I don't need your morality,' she said, glaring at him. She took another cigarette from the packet and lit it.

'Why?'

'Why do you think?' she snapped. 'It helps me forget how I've fucked up my life.'

'It doesn't work, though, does it?'

'No? I don't think about very much when I'm high. You should try it.'

'I have tried it,' he said. 'That's the reason I don't drink any more. It works for a while until it doesn't. And then it's much worse.'

'Please don't tell me you're in a programme?'

'AA,' Milton said. He smiled wryly.

'What's so funny?'

'That's the first time I've admitted it to anyone who wasn't already in the Rooms.'

'Yeah? Well, good for you, but I still think it's bullshit. There's no point trying to persuade me to do something stupid like that. The first thing you need is to want to stop, right?'

'Yes . . .'

'I don't want to stop.'

'You're not—'

'There's something else, Milton. The other reason I do it.' She took a deep breath. 'It's a palliative.'

'For what?'

'I have cancer.'

'Oh, shit. I'm sorry.'

'Don't be. I told you. I don't need your sympathy.'

He shifted uncomfortably; the conversation had veered hopelessly away from where he thought it might go. 'How bad is it?'

'Bad. Breast cancer, stage four. It's in my liver and my lungs.'

'Have you had treatment?'

She shrugged. 'What's the point?'

'So you haven't?'

She waved a hand disdainfully. 'There's a doctor I know, discreet if you pay him enough. He's given me two rounds of chemotherapy. I might've had a third, but I've run out of money. Don't do anything stupid like offer to pay for it. I'm all right with it. We're all going to die, Milton, especially people like us. I just know I'll be sooner than most.'

'How long do you have left?'

'He can't say for sure. All they can do is manage it now. No more than eighteen months.' She smiled bitterly. 'So I eat like shit and I smoke and I drink and when the pain gets too much, I smoke heroin so I can't feel it any more. And one day, when I can't take it any more, I'll shoot up enough to bring an end to it. You think about it from my point of view, it's not a bad way to go.'

Milton laid his hands flat on the table. 'What about your daughter?'

Her eyes flashed. *'Don't.'*

'You don't want to see her again? Before . . .'

'Before I die? Yes, Milton, of course I do. I want that more than anything. But if Control gets even the slightest hint that I'm in the country again, he is going to think I'm coming after him; and if he thinks that, she isn't safe. I can't take the risk. I can't go back. You see, Milton? This can't be fixed.'

He stared right into her face. 'No. You're wrong. Everything can be fixed.'

'Not this.'

'What about if I said I could get her back?'

37

They talked for another two hours. Milton didn't have a plan and so they worked it out on the fly.

'Where are the flash drives?' he asked her.

Beatrix paused.

'I've got almost as much of a reason to bring down Control as you do. This won't work if you don't trust me.'

'I know. But . . . I don't really know you, Milton, and that's my only leverage. If I let you have it and it goes wrong . . .'

'Come on, *think*. What's that leverage really worth? How much good has it done you?'

'And how would giving it to the Russians help me?'

'Who said that I was going to give it to them?'

'Then what?'

He rubbed his forehead with the palm of his hand. 'There are other ways to make this work.'

'It's in England.'

'Okay.'

'And so is my daughter. How are you going to get her? It's *England*. You can't go back, just like I can't go back. Control will kill you.'

'Someone has to go back. It might as well be me. I can't keep running forever.'

38

Anna insisted that she meet Beatrix. It was, she said tersely, a prerequisite for the continuation of the operation. Milton called Beatrix and they arranged a sit-down at the coffee shop. They took a table. Beatrix kept them waiting for thirty minutes and, when she finally arrived, she was wearing dark sunglasses and an impassive expression.

'Thank you for coming,' Anna said, trying to sound authoritative, but the effort was undermined by the tremors in her hand. The indignation with the way that Milton had manoeuvred her quickly disappeared as she sat between the two veteran assassins. Her confidence wilted and she fell back upon bravado. Milton was surprised to find himself sympathetic towards her. Seeing her flounder reminded him how young and inexperienced she was. He also felt regret at what he knew he was going to have to do once they were in England. He was sure now that this was her first solo operation and it was obvious that she was determined to do well. She was young and vigorous and desperate to impress Shcherbatov. It wasn't going to end up the way she wanted.

'Let's be quick,' Beatrix said. 'There are things we need to be doing.'

'I need to know what you have planned,' Anna said. 'If I'm not satisfied, we don't go any further.'

'I could just leave,' Beatrix replied. 'I can go wherever I want.'

'But he can't,' Anna remarked, gesturing towards Milton.

'What are you talking about? He can go wherever he wants.'

'Let me put it another way,' Anna said, managing to put a little irritation in her voice. 'You can both go wherever you want, whenever you want, but if Captain Milton cares about Captain Pope, you'll do this on my terms.'

'*I* don't care about him,' Beatrix said. 'I hardly know him, and it was a long time ago. You need me, and you'll need to do better than that.'

Anna's mouth opened and closed as she tried to find the proper retort and failed. She looked from Beatrix, still wearing her glasses, and turned to Milton, looking at her with amused forbearance. 'Captain Milton,' she said, floundering a little, 'I thought you said she was reliable?'

'She is,' he replied, and, turning to Beatrix, he added, 'Go easy on her. She's got her orders.'

Beatrix sat back and raised her hands in a gesture of helplessness. 'Fine. She's your problem, not mine.'

Milton leant forward and looked into Anna's face. 'The plan is this,' Milton said. 'Beatrix says that she can get you the evidence that the colonel needs for whatever it is he has planned for Control. She's going to tell me where to find it and I'm going to go and get it.'

'Why can't she go?'

'England isn't safe for her.'

'It's not safe for you.'

'It's a risk I'm prepared to take. The items are hidden. It doesn't have to be Beatrix who collects them. She just needs to tell me where they are.'

'And what about her? What does she do?'

'She's going to stay here.'

'And she'll give up her secrets just like that?' Anna looked at Beatrix again and said, accusatorially, 'What's in it for you?'

Beatrix sighed. Milton looked at her, and could see Anna's face reflected in the lenses of her glasses. 'We all have skin in the game here, don't we?' she said. 'Control needs to be out of the picture. The reason I can't go back is because of him. Same goes for Milton. And he's told me that your colonel has a hard-on for him. He'll be able to take him down with my evidence. We all win: your boss gets Control, Milton gets to go home, I get to go home.'

Anna didn't give up. 'Why can't you go back?'

'That's none of your business,' Beatrix said.

'I think it is.'

'He has my daughter. If I go back, and he knows about it, she isn't safe. All right? Is that a good enough reason for you?'

'Your daughter . . .'

'Anna,' Milton said, interrupting her. 'You don't need to trust her. You only need to trust me. And I'm prepared to go back to England because I believe that she has the evidence that you need and I am going to get it for you. If I'm wrong about her, it'll probably mean I end up getting shot. But I'm a good judge of character and I think I'm right. That should be good enough for Shcherbatov.' He paused and assessed her; she looked as if she was wrestling with a decision. 'Do you need to speak to him?'

She shook her head, frowning angrily. 'It's my operation,' she said. 'It's my decision.'

'So what are we going to do?'

'Fine.' She clenched her jaw. 'We go to London.'

PART 5
LONDON

39

Milton stood on the edge of the small airfield, looking at the rows of planes lined up at the side of the grass strip. It had been a long day and a half of travel and there was still more to come. Anna had obtained two tickets for them on Emirates from Hong Kong to Paris Charles de Gaulle and, from there, they'd driven north to Brittany.

The atmosphere between the two of them had been tense for the first few hours. She was still angry and embarrassed about the way that Milton had waylaid her and the inflammatory meeting with Beatrix hadn't helped. It was pride. Milton knew that she needed to reassert her authority again and so he played along; he needed her on his side for at least the next couple of days.

They had discussed the best way to get into the country when they returned to the hotel. Milton had explained that there was no way that he would be able to get in through the airports, the tunnel or the ports. He knew that his likeness would have been circulated and that it would take moments for an alert to be sounded, and moments after that for armed police to have them face down on the ground.

Anna wasn't fazed. She had another method prepared. There was a private airfield on the outskirts of Lannion that local enthusiasts used to explore the north coast of France. There was a small café that served croissants and coffee and they had met their pilot there. He was a quiet, taciturn man, and, when he spoke, it was with an English accent. The man had explained that he had flown south from Bournemouth on the pretext of a pleasure flight and that he was cleared to return by the end of the day. He was an SVR man, Milton assumed. It was not a surprise. The agency had already demonstrated the breadth of its reach and it clearly was not beyond them to be able to activate a pilot in the south of England to fly them across the channel.

'Where are you planning to land?' Milton asked as they walked across the facility to the Cessna Skyhawk that had been wheeled out of the line and readied for take-off.

'Back to Bournemouth,' the man said.

'We will drive from there to London,' Anna added. 'Will that work?'

'If you can get me into the country, I can handle the rest,' Milton said.

The pilot opened the cabin door and pulled himself inside. Anna followed him. Milton paused for a moment, taking a final look at the airstrip. There had been a number of moments over the last week that could have been described as points of no return. This was another, and the most significant yet. He knew that once he was inside the country, it would be difficult for him to get out again. He had been running away from the

Group for months and now he would voluntarily be making it much simpler for them to find him.

He entertained the thought, briefly, that he should turn away from the plane, make his way back to the autoroute, put out his thumb and hitch to Paris. It wasn't too late. He dismissed the notion as quickly as it had formed. That would mean Pope's death and he knew he would not be able to bear that on his conscience. And he had promised Beatrix his help, too. He couldn't let her down. His options were circumscribed and it was with that knowledge, and misgivings that what he was doing was still a mistake, that he reached up for the sill of the door and hauled himself inside the cabin.

*　*　*

The flight was easy. The conditions were perfect and, save a little turbulence as they descended over the south coast to the airstrip at Bournemouth airport, it passed off without incident. The pilot was a member of Bournemouth Flying Club. Like many of the other members of the club, he had a history of return trips to France and there was nothing about this trip that excited the interest of Customs and Excise. His flight details had recorded that the Cessna was carrying three passengers on departure from the UK and there were three passengers upon its return. He taxied the plane to its parking spot and all three disembarked. There was no official attention. The pilot went to file his papers with Customs; Milton and Anna took the car that was waiting for them in the car park and set off for London.

'What are you going to do?' she asked him as he drove north.

'I'm going to get your evidence.'

'And then?'

'And then you can get us back into France and we can go and give it to the colonel.'

'And it is in her old house?'

'That's what she said.'

'I'll come with you.'

'No you won't.'

'You're not leaving me out again . . .'

'I'm going to have to break in and get it.'

'You think I haven't done that before?'

He did, but he said, 'I'm sure you have, but I work best alone. You'll get in my way. This isn't going to work if we get caught, is it?' He looked across at her; she was frowning. 'Look, Anna, I'm not going to try to pull a trick.'

'Like before?'

He ignored that. 'What am I going to do? It isn't as if I've got any friends here, is it? Who am I going to ask for help?'

'I realise that.'

'I'm here, aren't I? Have I done anything to make you think I'm not going to follow through on this?'

She didn't answer that.

'And I'm not going to. The colonel has worked me into a corner. I don't have any options other than to co-operate.'

40

Milton drove them to the Docklands Holiday Inn. He told Anna to take a room and wait for him to return. He said he would be back later that night. She looked uncomfortable, but he had persuaded her that the only way for him to collect the evidence was alone and, after a moment of grumbling dissatisfaction, she conceded the point.

He took the tube to Liverpool Street and emerged into the blustery afternoon. It was just before three and the station concourse was busy with workers taking late lunches. He rode the escalator to street level, uncomfortably aware of the armed police stationed on the balcony, machine guns cradled carefully as they observed the busy comings and goings below.

Milton left the shelter of the wide awning that stretched out across the station entrance and into the spitting rain beyond. He took an eastbound bus and settled down for the short drive into the East End. The bus rumbled down the Kingsland Road, past the fried chicken shops, the money exchangers, the halal butchers and the charity shops, past the shabby bedsits above the shops that offered views of grim and brutal lives through their first-floor windows. A clutch of young girls climbed to the top deck and went to the back seat, taking out their smartphones, one of them playing the latest R&B through her phone's sibilant speaker.

Milton ignored the distraction. He was staring out of the window, only half aware of where he was, and thinking back to the last time he had visited the area, days after he had told Control that he wanted out.

He thought of Elijah and Sharon Warriner, of the confrontation with Number Twelve that had left him with a bullet in his shoulder and poor Derek Rutherford – the boxing instructor who had tried to help Elijah had met – with one in his head. He thought of the riots that had disfigured these streets and, as he saw the groups of shiftless kids loitering on street corners, and felt the almost tangible buzz of aggression in the atmosphere, he didn't doubt that the tinder was still dry, and with the right spark it could all start burning again.

Taking out his phone, Milton opened the map. He had nearly reached the stop he remembered from before and so he rang the bell, climbed down the stairs and disembarked. There was an arcade of shops and he stopped in the small hardware shop to buy a chisel, the bored-looking owner trying without success to engage him in conversation. There was a pharmacy next door; Milton went inside and bought a box of latex gloves. Back outside, he removed two pairs from the box. He stuffed them into his pockets and dropped the box in the nearest bin.

The main road was busy with traffic, a building site representing a half-hearted stab at regeneration, but a few hundred yards to the south was an area of Victorian housing that had been appropriated by the middle class. The area was close to the city and the houses were solid and pleasant; Milton knew that it was an expensive place to live.

He followed the map until he reached Lavender Grove, a charming street overhung with trees. The houses were neat and tidy and the narrow walled gardens that separated the terrace from the pavement were all carefully tended. Beatrix Rose had lived at number thirty. Milton walked down the opposite side of the street, observing the house with a careful eye. The doorway was painted bright red and the brass door furniture was well polished. There was a bicycle in the garden, propped up against the side of the house, and a blind in the top right window was pulled down.

He walked the length of the street, observing the little details: the car that pulled into the kerb outside number eighteen; the open door at number twenty-three, a builder inside sanding the exposed floorboards; the elderly woman with a shopping trolley opening the gate of number twenty-six. Milton reached the end of the road, crossed over to the other side and turned back, checking for additional activity. It was all reasonably quiet; the people who lived here would be at work. It was as much as could be hoped for in a busy London residential street in the middle of the day.

Milton reached into his pocket and pulled out the latex gloves. He put them on.

He arrived at number thirty again. With a final check that he wasn't observed, he reached down for the handle of the freshly painted metal gate, opened it and approached the front door. He knocked, two times, and paused, straining his ears. He waited thirty seconds and then dropped to his knees, pushing open the letterbox and looking inside: there was no sign that anyone was home. He checked up and down the street again. Nothing.

Beatrix had said that the door had always been secured with a single mortise lock; he hoped that hadn't changed. He reached into his pocket for the chisel, shoved it between the door and the jamb, right over the spot where the lock bolt inserted into the box keep, and pulled it back, hard. The door splintered and the bolt popped free. Milton shouldered the door to force it the rest of the way open, stepped quickly inside and pushed it closed behind him. It wouldn't close properly now that he had damaged it and so he pulled across a large vase that held umbrellas and jammed it against the door.

He listened.

Nothing.

He moved quickly, ignoring the doorways to the sitting room, the kitchen and the downstairs toilet and climbed the stairs to the floor above. Magnolia painted walls, framed prints on the wall. He registered the details peripherally, gaining the landing, passing the open door to the family bathroom and opening the door to the main bedroom. The blind over the window was suffused with dim sunlight, just enough to see, and it revealed a messy room: the bed was unmade, pairs of shoes were stacked up against a wall, clothes spilled out of a wicker basket.

Milton moved to the corner of the room next to the window, knelt down and slid his fingers between the carpet and the floorboards. He pulled hard, popping the carpet tacks, and hauled the corner of the carpet back so that he could see the boards beneath. He took the chisel and drove the point into the spot where two boards were nailed to the joist, and yanked back, hard. The wood was old and brittle, scarred with woodworm, and it splintered easily. He inserted the chisel again and prised up a second board, then dropped the tool and used his hands to remove it.

There was a small, waterproof freezer bag in the cavity below, resting on the plasterboard ceiling. Milton reached down and pulled it out. There were six USB flash drives inside. He put the drives into his pocket, replaced the boards, covered them with the carpet, collected his chisel and made his way back downstairs again. He lifted the vase out of the way, opened the door and stepped back into the front garden. The road was still quiet. The door drifted open behind him and Milton slammed it, the splintered wood grinding together and holding the door shut. He opened the gate, stepped through, and walked quickly back up the road and away.

41

Control's driver was waiting for him next to the Cenotaph in Whitehall. It was a blustery, overcast day, the late afternoon turning into evening, and he paused in the shelter of the entrance to the Ministry building to turn up the collar of his overcoat and open his umbrella. The weather had been like this for a week, and now the gutters were swollen with run-off water and pedestrians hurried to their destinations as the rain lashed around them.

Control stepped out from the shelter and a gust of wind caught the umbrella and turned it inside out. Cursing to himself, he hurried down the street, opened the door of the Jaguar and got inside.

The driver asked him where he would like to go.

'The flat,' Control said. 'Don't hang about.'

The driver put the car into gear, pulled into the traffic and headed towards the towers and minarets of the Houses of Parliament. Control looked up at the big Union Jack snapping from its flagpole high above, the pennant ripped back and forth by the gusting wind, and then at the purple-black of the glowering skies behind it. The forecasters were predicting another week of storms. Control's country house was in a Wiltshire village that was bisected by a river that carved its course through the valley; he had been too busy to go home since last weekend, but his wife had reported that the water was in full spate, and there was some concern that it was close to bursting its banks. It would flood the orchard at the bottom of their garden. She had been very concerned when she had explained the situation. Control had made all the right noises, but he had too much to think about in London to worry about that.

The meeting had been called on short notice. The Foreign Secretary had chaired it and he had been joined by the heads of MI5 and MI6. The mood had been pensive. They still had no idea what had happened to Number One. It had been almost a week now; protocol required them to assume the worst. The Foreign Secretary had been furious, but Control had anticipated his reaction and was not caught out by it. It was a risk that came with the territory in which the Group operated, he had explained. Agents were lost; that could not be avoided. Control was measured and calm and had explained what might have happened and what would happen next with patience and tact. The Foreign Secretary was a civilian with no operational experience. That was the problem with politicians; they could not possibly begin to understand the exigencies of his work. The man needed careful handling. The whole Milton debacle had been a challenge to navigate and he had only just emerged on the other side of that, and this new setback would just be a question of educating him into the realities of life in the field.

The bottom line was brutally simple: these things happened.

Pope had been promoted to Number One after Milton had disappeared. The two of them had been friends. Control remembered that they had served together in Northern Ireland at the beginning of their careers. Despite that, he trusted Pope. He had led the team that he had sent to Mexico to bring Milton back and there was no suggestion that its failure had anything to do with his leadership.

The meeting had dragged on. The Foreign Secretary had asked what was likely to happen to Pope if he had been captured and they had debated the possibilities for a while, but Control found the discussion tedious and otiose; he had already jettisoned him. He was dead. Even if he had been captured and even if he could have been exchanged for one of the Russian spies that they had swept up over the years, he would still be useless to him. Pope was burnt: a busted flush. He was finished and, as such, Control would waste no more time or effort on him. It was a difficult job that he did, he reminded himself, and there was no place for sentiment.

The Foreign Secretary had sat at the head of the table, an expression of supercilious disdain on his face and, when the discussion about Pope drew to its conclusion, he had removed his spectacles and tapped them on the table.

'Of course,' he had said, 'we understand that we are going to lose agents from time to time. Natural erosion, as you say. Can't be helped. But this is the second time in a year. If it was just the once, well, we could accept that and move on. But it isn't. What about Milton?'

Milton.

The thought of him had angered Control and now that anger returned like the echo of thunder. Pope's loss was excusable. It was regrettable, but, as he had made plain, it was a risk that went with the territory. But Milton was different. That was a loss that would stay on his résumé, a stain that would always be there to diminish his many other successes. He blamed himself for what had happened. There had been signs, plenty of signs, but Milton was such a brilliant agent that he had wilfully ignored all of them. That had been a critical mistake. He should have put the failsafes into motion as soon as he had entertained the first suspicion that he was breaking down. He should have issued a file on him, a file with red borders, and given it to one of the other agents to execute. Callan could have done it; the boy was keen. *That* would have put an end to months of blame and recrimination. *That* would have preserved his reputation.

Control had only made one other mistake like that in all the years that he had been in command of the Group and he had managed Beatrix Rose much more successfully than he had managed John Milton.

So far.

Pedestrians swilled around the car as the lights that faced the Houses of Parliament went to red.

Milton.

He felt his temper kindling.

He needed distraction. He opened his briefcase, taking out the latest files that had been assigned to the Group and spread them out on his lap. The Jaguar broke out of the jam that had gathered at the lights, turned left onto Westminster Bridge, and accelerated away.

42

Control owned a flat in Chelsea. He had purchased it ten years ago when he had started to spend more time in the city than at home. He was getting home later and later and it made sense to have a *pied-à-terre* to which he could retire when long nights were necessary.

The driver pulled up to the side of the road, got out and opened the door for him. Control bid him goodnight and crossed the pavement to the front door. He fumbled in his pocket for the key, pressed it into the lock and opened the door. The driver, who was armed, waited until he was inside and then drove away.

What a day.

Control deactivated the alarm, took off his overcoat, hung his umbrella on the hatstand and removed his shoes. He massaged the soles of his aching feet and then stood before the mirror. He was dressed immaculately, as ever, in a well-tailored suit that showed an inch of creamy white cuff. His regimental tie was fastened with a brass pin. He was of late middle age, of average height, a little overweight, his hair thinning at the crown. He was not the sort of man who would excite attention. He was as anonymous as a provincial accountant. Perfect for the job that he was asked to do.

He rubbed his eyes. He had been up since five and he was tired. He needed a drink. Taking off his suit jacket, he hung it on the bannister of the stairs leading up to the two bedrooms on the first floor and went through into the sitting room. There was a drinks trolley pushed back against the wall and he took a bottle of Scotch through into the kitchen and poured himself a generous measure. He looked out of the window into the garden beyond. Night had drawn in properly now, and, as he looked out onto the narrow strip of lawn and the rear of the terrace opposite, with the slate roofs, the chimneys and the satellite dishes, the sky flashed with a pulse of lightning. He put the glass to his lips and sipped, the liquid warming his gullet as rain started to fall, lashing the window, and, in the distance, a peal of thunder rolled across the city.

The fridge was well stocked with ready meals. He took out a chicken curry, removed the cardboard sleeve, slid it into the microwave and set the timer for five minutes. The machine hummed as the platter rotated and, soon, the smell of the food filled the kitchen. He would eat and then review the files he had brought home, perhaps with the benefit of another drink.

He took his glass and the bottle back into the sitting room. It was almost ten o'clock, and it was his habit to listen to *The World Tonight* on Radio Four.

The room was dark and he stooped at the standard lamp.

He was fumbling for the switch when the light on the other side of the room switched on.

The figure of a man was silhouetted in the armchair.

'Hello, Control.'

John Milton was sitting there, unmoving, watching him. His face was cast in shadow by the lamp just behind his shoulder.

Control's stomach suddenly felt turned inside out.

'You must have known I'd come back for you one day?'

Control couldn't look directly at him without squinting into the light. Milton would have planned it that way.

'I don't—'

Milton held up a hand to stop him and then leant forward so that Control could see him more clearly. He was dressed all in black: black jacket, black jeans and a pair of black boots. He was wearing latex gloves on his hands and he held a revolver in his right hand.

'Before we get started, let me set a couple of things out. First, I've been waiting for you a little while. More than long enough to find both of your panic alarms. They're disabled now, so don't think you can call for help. You can't. It's just me and you. Second, there was a pistol in the drawer over there, too. This one.' He held up the Jericho 941F semi-automatic. 'It wasn't loaded, but I found where you keep the ammunition and it is now.'

Control's knees felt like water. 'Can I sit down?'

Milton waved the gun at the settee.

'What do you want?'

'A discussion.'

'About what? About you?'

Milton turned his head a little and Control could see that his thin lips had formed a cold smile. 'No. Not about me. A few other things.'

'Such as?'

'Let's start with Michael Pope.'

Control measured that. 'All right,' he said.

The microwave pinged in the kitchen. Control jumped, but Milton didn't take his eyes off him. This must be what it felt like for those men and women that he sent his agents to neutralise. Control's authority, his position, his years of experience; they were all useless in the face of the hard-faced killer sitting opposite him.

And Milton *was* a killer. Cold-blooded and lethally efficient. No one knew that better than Control. John Milton was the best assassin he had ever worked with. The absolute best; no one else came anywhere close. He had been Number One, after all. He was the most relentless, the most ruthless, the most deadly operative he had ever sent into the field.

Milton sat back in the chair and the shadows fell back across his face again. 'Do you know what's happened to him?'

'He was on assignment. South of France. We haven't heard from him for days.'

'Who was the target?'

'I can't tell you that.'

'Was it Pascha Shcherbatov?'

That took him by surprise. 'I-I-' he stammered.

'He sends his regards.'

Control put the empty glass down on the side table; his hand was shaking and it rattled against the wood. He was already nervous and the direction the conversation was taking made him feel even worse. 'You've met him?'

'A few days ago. Pope is alive. Shcherbatov has him. He used him to get to me.'

'How do they know about you?'

'That I don't know,' he said, drily. 'But they knew quite a lot. If you asked me to guess, I'd say that you're employing one of his agents.'

'Don't be ridiculous.'

'He knew Pope was coming after him. And he knew where to find me. Draw the dots, Control.'

'So what did he want?'

'We'll get to that. I want you to tell me about Beatrix Rose first.'

That surprised him. The conversation wasn't following a path he could predict and he needed time to think. He absently knocked back the last of his drink. He held the glass up and said, 'I don't know about you, but I—'

'Stay there. You need to take this seriously.'

'I am taking it seriously.'

'No distractions. I wasn't born yesterday.' Milton tapped his index finger on the barrel of the gun. 'So – Beatrix Rose.'

'What do you want to know?'

'I never found out what happened to her.'

'You know the procedure: minimum information. You didn't need to know.'

He brought up the gun. 'And now I do.'

Control waved his hand in the air before his face. 'There was an assignment, just after you were transferred, I believe, and she was compromised. She didn't report afterwards. We assumed what we would always assume in the circumstances: K.I.A.'

Milton leant forward again to stare at him, the shadows reaching down his face like daggers. 'This is going to be so much easier if you tell me the truth.'

Control felt panic closing around him. He had no idea what he should say, what Milton did and did not know.

'Let me help you out. I know she's not dead.'

'How could you possibly know that?'

'Because I went to see her after I saw Shcherbatov.'

'Where?'

He smiled and shook his head. 'You don't need to know where. But you might as well assume she told me everything. I know what you were doing then, when she disappeared. I know that you'd been prostituting yourself for years. I know all about the deal you thought you were doing with Anastasia Semenko. I know that you thought that she was an arms dealer looking for a way in with the Syrians. I know that she was introduced to you by the Iraqis that you'd already been working with, although you didn't know that they were also working with the Russians. I know that you didn't know that the Iraqis were in the habit of selling useful information to the Russians. I know that Semenko paid you because you said you could make an introduction with Assad's regime. I know that the Russians had you exactly where they wanted you. I know that the meeting Semenko and Shcherbatov were going to on the day that she died was with you. And I know that you sent us after them because you couldn't afford to let them live.

Shcherbatov told me everything and Beatrix Rose confirmed it. How long did it take you to find out he survived?'

Control glared at him with sullen frustration. 'We thought he'd drowned in the river, but then he popped up again in Moscow a week later.'

Milton chuckled, humourlessly. 'Did you know that he was romantically involved with Semenko?'

'No, I didn't.'

'You can't blame him for hating you. He wants to disgrace you. And then he wants to kill you.'

Control felt a bead of sweat as it rolled out of his scalp and traced a slow line down his forehead. 'Why are you telling me this?'

'I'm getting to that,' he said. 'Do you want to reconsider what you told me about Beatrix?'

Control looked at the gun in Milton's hand and swallowed hard. 'It's true about Semenko. They trapped me. They were ready to flip me. Can you imagine how dangerous that would have been for the state?'

'Best you don't try to justify what you did,' he warned. 'I'm not in the mood.'

'Rose found the evidence in the car that they were using to blackmail me. Photographs, financial records. She brought in the pictures and showed me. I tried to brush it off, but I knew it wouldn't wash. She'd guessed what had happened and that didn't leave me with any choice.'

'Meaning?'

'Meaning I sent agents to dispose of her.'

It was a flippant choice of synonym and he regretted it at once. He saw Milton stiffen and the gun jerked.

'And?' he said.

'And that was a fuck-up, too. Chisolm shot her husband and Rose stabbed her in the throat. Spenser took her daughter and she fled. I have no idea where she went. We never heard from her again.'

'Because she knows that if she comes after you, you have her girl. An insurance policy.'

'She was taken into protective custody.'

'Come on,' Milton snapped angrily. 'Don't waste my time.'

'There might have been something about using the girl to concentrate the mother's mind.'

Milton passed the gun from his right hand to his left.

'What's going on, Milton?'

Milton told him. He spoke for five minutes, explaining how Anna Kushchyenko had picked him up in Texas and flown him to Moscow, how he had been taken to see Shcherbatov and how he had shown him Pope. Milton said that Pope was sick and Control feigned concern. Milton explained that he had agreed to work with them so that he could buy a little time to think of something better. The Russians had located Beatrix Rose and he had gone to speak to her.

'Why does he want her?' Control asked.

'Because he wanted to talk to her about what happened that afternoon,' Milton said. 'He knows you didn't get everything she took from the car. She copied the drives. She hid them before she came to see you. I've got them now. I collected them this afternoon before I came here.' He reached his right hand into a pocket and retrieved a clear bag with six flash drives in it.

'It would be better to give those to me,' he said.

'I'm sure you'd like that.'

There was panic in his voice. 'You're going to give them to the Russians?'

'Of course not. I needed an insurance policy of my own. This is it. And just so it's clear, I've downloaded these myself. They'll be attached to emails that I have set up to send automatically in the future. Unless I delete them, they'll go far and wide: government, the press, everywhere I can think of. It's my dead man's switch.'

'So what do you want?'

'First, I want Beatrix's daughter. She has grandparents in Somerset. You're going to deliver her to them. I want fresh passports for both her and her mother.'

'I can do that.'

'And two million dollars paid into a bank account of my designation.'

He bit his lip. 'Two million?'

'That's right.'

'That's not so easy . . .'

'I need the Russian girl put under surveillance. She's Shcherbatov's proxy. She came into the country with me and she should be at the Holiday Inn in the Docklands. She's expecting me to bring the drives back tonight and I'm guessing if I'm not back by midnight, she'll sound the alarm and that will be that for Pope. You need to get on that right away.'

'Fine. Anything else?'

'The third thing: you're going to help me go and get Pope.'

'How am I going to do that?'

'A six-man team, full load out, logistic support.'

'Are you mad? Pope is in Russia, man. We can't send six of you to conduct an operation on Russian soil.'

'Yes you can.'

'No . . .'

'The Russians will help.'

'You're going to have to explain that.'

'I know they asked you to go after Shcherbatov for them. Pope told me. You want to tell me why?'

Control felt helpless. Milton knew everything; he had no cards to play. 'Fine. The colonel has gone rogue. He's old-school, from before the fall of the Wall. He hates the west, and he hates the thought that the motherland is pandering to it. They want him out of the way. They can't be seen to conduct an operation against one of their own, especially on home turf, and he's been around a long time. He has too much on the Kremlin for them to risk getting rid of him themselves and it all going wrong, especially as it appears that he is a hard man to kill. They knew we had assets who could do it, he put himself into a position where it was possible and so we assigned him a file.'

Milton interjected. 'Having the man we sent to kill him in his custody doesn't do the Kremlin any good, does it? How long do you think it'll take someone like Shcherbatov to break Pope and find out that his own people asked us to send him?'

'Pope's strong. But . . .'

'But we both know he'll break eventually. No. You can persuade them to do this, Control. You tell them we'll go in, we'll get Pope and we'll take out Shcherbatov. Properly, this time. You've tried twice already. I'll make sure it's done right.'

Control furrowed his brow. It might work, he thought. 'Maybe,' he said.

'A team of agents of my choosing, under my command.'

Control was about to rule out Milton's involvement, but then he caught himself. There was another way he could play this; perhaps he could come out on top in the whole deal after all. 'Maybe,' he said. 'I'll need to think about it.'

'That's what I want,' he said. 'There's no negotiation and the alternative is bad for you. It's your call.'

Milton stood. He obscured the light from the lamp and Control could see his face properly for the first time: the implacable powder-blue eyes; the horizontal scar from his cheek to the start of his nose; the whiteness outlining his lips. There was no softness in that face. No pity.

'What happens to the information about me?'

'If you do as you're told? Nothing.'

'You'll return it?'

'No. I just won't publicise it.'

'This will need discussing.'

'With who? You can't take this to the government. It's your call. Pick the girl up tonight. If she reports I'm not playing ball, then this is all moot and our deal is off. The first priority is to manage her. And then you need to sort out Rose's daughter.

You can do that tonight, too. I want her to be on her way to her grandparents by noon.'

'You think it's as easy as that? Just make a few calls?'

'I don't care how easy or how difficult it is. You just need to get it done.' Milton crossed the room until he was standing next to him; he knelt down so that their faces were on the same level. 'You know me well enough, Control. You know me better than almost anyone. And you know that if I say I'm going to do something, I do it.'

'I know.'

'So here it is, just in case you need reminding: if anything happens to Beatrix Rose, I'll be back. If I get a whiff that you're about to do something I don't like, I'll be back. That's a promise. I'll be back with your gun, in this room, waiting for you. You'll never see me coming. You know who I am, Control, don't you?'

He felt his throat thicken. 'Yes,' he said. 'I do.'

'I'm a bad man, Control. I'm a bad man who kills bad men. And you are one of the worst.'

43

Anna had spent a long and tedious night waiting for John Milton to return.

She had drawn a bath and soaked in it for an hour, thinking about the Englishman and questioning, once again, whether she had erred in allowing him to make his way into London alone. Colonel Shcherbatov had granted her the latitude to judge how to proceed; he had trained her, nurtured her career over many years, and he trusted her. She was as devoted to him as a daughter to her father and the thought of letting him down was abhorrent to her.

It was difficult to argue with her performance so far. Persuading Milton to come to Russia had been difficult, but she had managed to do that. Delivering him to the colonel had been a challenge, too, and she had managed that. She had helped him to find Beatrix Rose, managed him as he persuaded her to assist their cause and delivered him back to the United Kingdom. None of it had been easy, but, here she was, seemingly with his co-operation assured and waiting for him to return with the evidence that the colonel had said would be of priceless importance in his fight against the imperialists. Nurturing the operation to a successful conclusion would be a coup and she knew that he would be grateful.

That was all the motivation that Anna needed.

She visited an internet café after her bath. It was a small operation at the back of a Polish grocery store and the proprietor didn't even look at her twice as she bought a token for an hour's use and settled before the screen in a wooden cubicle that would guarantee her privacy. She created a new Gmail account and posted a message on the bulletin board of a Justin Bieber fan site. It was a bland message, seemingly in tune with the rest of the comments, but the board was monitored and her message would be delivered to the colonel. The coded message reported that the operation was proceeding as planned and that she anticipated leaving the country with the package they had come to collect tomorrow.

She logged out of the PC and went back outside. It was a brisk night, with a cool breeze blowing in off the darkened river, and she decided to go for a walk for some exercise and fresh air. She ambled along the quay at one of the nearby yacht basins. The wind was cold and there were only a few people out. She saw a man leaning against the metal rails that protected the drop into the water below, gazing out at the yachts moored out on a floating jetty, their rigging rattling in the breeze. She walked beyond the man, realising, but much too late, that something about him was not right. She turned just as he had started after her, closing the distance in a couple of broad strides, taking her arm just above the elbow and impelling her towards a car at the kerb.

'Don't make a scene, miss,' he said in a quiet, firm voice.

'Who are you?'

'British intelligence. Afraid we need to hold onto you for a while.'

44

Milton was driven to RAF Northolt. Group Fifteen used the facility when agents were not able to fly commercially and he was very familiar with it. The driver swept off the main road, paused to register their credentials at the gatehouse, and then sped through the wire mesh gate as it was drawn aside for them. He drove past the row of buildings that housed the base's administrative and engineering staff and out to a single-storey building right on the edge of the runway itself. A Hercules C-130 aircraft was being fuelled nearby.

It was just after dawn.

Milton got out of the car and went into the building.

Control was waiting for him. There were five others there, too. He recognised one of them very well and the other three were familiar.

'Captain Milton,' Control said stiffly. 'Are you ready to go?'

'I am,' he said.

'You know everyone?'

'Well enough,' Milton said.

He looked them over and put names, and assignations, to faces.

Number Two was Corporal Spenser: short, bald and heavily muscled.

Number Six was Corporal Blake: darker skinned, foreign, perhaps, although Milton did not know enough about him to say from where.

Number Eight was Lance Corporal Hammond: female; early thirties; five eight; black hair, cut short; compact and powerfully built. Milton had surrendered to her in El Patrón's mansion. She had a reputation for callousness.

Number Nine was Sergeant Underwood: the tallest of the four, well over six foot; broad shoulders; old acne scars scattered across his nose and cheeks.

Control turned to the final man. 'And Lance Corporal Callan.'

'Yes,' Milton said. 'Number Twelve.'

'Number Ten now,' Control said, 'at least until Captain Pope is recovered.'

Callan was tall and slender and strikingly handsome. His hair was in tight curls and so blond that it was almost white. His skin was pale, almost alabaster. There was a cruelty to his lips and unfeeling eyes that Milton remembered very well indeed. He had executed Derek Rutherford in cold blood and then shot Milton in the shoulder; Milton had overcome him and put a bullet in his knee. According to Pope, he had been keen to end him there and then when they captured him in Mexico.

'They were all in Juàrez,' Milton said.

'That's right.'

'They'll need to do better this time.'

'We found you,' Spenser said. 'We took you.'

'You did. And you took out a dozen cartel soldiers doing it and, yes, that was impressive. But then you let an overweight Mexican police officer on his last day undo all of that good work. So you can count me not especially impressed. Shcherbatov's men won't be as easy as the cartel. They'll be well trained, well equipped and they might be expecting us. If you're as lax as that when we go in tomorrow, I guarantee you one thing: we'll all get shot.'

Spenser glared at him but said nothing. Milton felt Callan's eyes burning into his back, too, and knew that he would have to proceed very carefully if he wanted to get out of Russia in one piece.

'Shall we discuss the plan?' Control suggested.

Milton held Spenser's stare long enough to let him know that he was far from intimidated; Number Two broke first and looked away. 'Go on,' Milton said.

'The Russians are going to give us some low-visibility help.'

'Why would they do something like that?' Underwood asked.

'Shcherbatov is off the reservation. There could be an incident if we don't get Pope back and they know that is not in their interests right now. They won't support you if you get into trouble, but they don't mind making it easier for you to get to where you need to go.'

'Go on, then,' Milton said. 'I'm all ears.'

There was an iPad on the table. Control selected a map of Russia and they all gathered around it. 'You're going out in the

Hercules. It has just enough range to get you to Kubinka air base, south-east of Moscow. You'll be travelling under the pretext of a military exchange: senior members of the RAF flying in for a joint exercise with their Russian equivalents. Happens reasonably frequently. Won't draw unnecessary attention.'

'And from Kubinka?'

'The Hercules will be refuelled. You'll head north and do a HALO jump twenty clicks south of Plyos. And then the Hercules turns around and heads back to Kubinka.'

'Air traffic control?'

'We're told that they will be looking the other way.'

Hammond looked sceptical. 'We're dropping twenty clicks from the target?'

'That's right.'

'In the Russian winter?'

'You'll be taking transport on the Hercules. The Russians are arranging it.'

'What do we know about the target?'

'It's a dacha,' Milton explained. He didn't have to work hard to remember it; he had a photographic memory for tactical information and he relayed it quickly and easily. 'Three storeys, walled, two internal courtyards. Good security.'

'How many?'

'I'd guess a dozen.'

'Any good?'

'Spetsnaz. Very good.'

'Armed with what?'

'AN-94s and AS Vals. Like I said, they're proper soldiers.'

Milton gave them all the additional information that he thought might be helpful: the internal layout of the dacha, the basement cell where it was likely Pope would be held.

'And you're sure Pope is still there?' Control said.

'I'm sure enough.'

'How sure?'

'Eighty per cent.'

Hammond shook her head. 'So twenty per cent says this is us putting our necks on the line for nothing?'

Milton stared her down. 'And eighty per cent says that you're not.'

She turned to Control and protested, 'We need better odds for something like this.'

Control regarded Milton carefully. 'Are you going to tell me why you think he's still there?'

'No,' he said. 'I have intelligence. But you're going to have to trust me.'

'All right,' Control said. 'I'm happy to proceed on that basis.'

Milton knew that he had no room for manoeuvre. He had evidence on Control that would have him locked up in an MI6 Black Site for the rest of his natural life. He had no choice but to give the operation the green light.

Spenser pointed down at the map. 'Say we manage to get in, find the dacha, take out the guards and get Pope. How do we get out again?'

Control dragged his finger down the screen, adjusting the map. 'You make your way south to Privolzhsk . . . here. Sixteen kilometres. Provided you get there in one piece, the Russians

243

will give you a ride back to Kubinka and you'll fly out again on the Hercules from there.'

Milton looked at the five soldiers, gauging their reaction to the plan. They did not look impressed, but there was little to be done about that. He would be able to fill them in on the smaller details en route, but there was no way round their obvious antipathy and suspicion towards him. That was something that he would have to live with.

45

The four Allison AE turboprops were fired up and the six-bladed propellors started to spin. Milton strapped himself into his seat and prepared for the flight. He needed something to distract himself and so he took out his Sig Sauer P226 and started to disassemble it. He released the magazine, pulled the slide, checked it was unloaded, separated the slide from the frame and took out the recoil spring. He removed the barrel from the slide and then, using a cotton bud and a small pot of oil, he cleaned and lubricated it.

It was a ritual that he had followed throughout his career, especially when he was facing a situation that concerned him. That word, concern, didn't quite do justice to what he was now proposing to do. He was going to parachute into Russia and then trek across the frozen tundra to a confrontation with Russian special forces where they would be outnumbered and outgunned, with no guarantee that the man they were going to rescue would even be there.

He emptied the magazine, counted all the ammo and slotted them all back again. The cabin of the Hercules was large and sparse, the cargo bay empty, with temporary chairs screwed into their housings. The agents were going through their own routines: reading, listening to music, looking out of the tiny porthole windows as the buildings at the edge of the runway accelerated into an indistinct blur.

He didn't trust Control. There was nothing to say that he wouldn't call Milton's bluff and there would be nothing he could do if he did. The other agents had made their disdain for Milton obvious and there was no doubt in his mind that they would shoot him if given half the chance.

Callan turned to look at him and, noticing that he was watching him, held his gaze.

Milton looked away.

He was not among friends.

As the Hercules reached the end of the runway and lumbered into the air, Milton started to put the gun back together.

PART 6
RUSSIA

46

The six-minute call.

The ramp of the aircraft opened, slowly lowering and letting moonlight and fresh air spill into the darkened cabin of the plane. Milton used the fabric ties attached to the walls of the plane to pull himself upright and took a step forwards. They were up high, thirty thousand feet, and the landscape below was indistinct. Milton was wearing arctic battle gear: his field jacket had a hood concealed in a zipper pocket at the back of the collar, four large cargo pockets and a double zipper. He had buttoned in a separate Gore-Tex liner for additional warmth, he was wearing polypropylene knit undergarments and full-face goggles over a balaclava that was unrolled all the way down to his throat. Right now, he was breathing pure oxygen through a mask to prevent nitrogen bubbles forming in his bloodstream. He stared out of the open end of the plane. It was minus forty outside and, were it not for the goggles, his eyes would have frozen instantly.

The jumpmaster signalled that they were ready to start the jump. Milton stood back as they released the drogue parachute that was attached to the first of the three snowmobiles on which they had stowed the rest of their gear. The chute snapped open and dragged the snowmobile backwards. It clicked across the metal rollers that were arranged across the width of the cabin, started to pick up speed as it rolled down the ramp and then disappeared out the back of the plane. They opened the chutes on the second and third snowmobiles and watched as they followed the first into the night. The plan was to drop their vehicles and gear first and then have the agents follow behind. Milton watched as the three main parachutes opened and the snowmobiles started their slow, gentle descent onto the snowy plains below.

The plan was simple enough. The Russians had permitted the C-130 free passage into their airspace. It had taken four hours to reach Kubinka. The Hercules had been refuelled and the Russians had loaded the three snowmobiles. They had been on the ground for an hour, long enough for Milton to stretch his legs and smoke a couple of cigarettes before they took off again. The jump point was over the horizon from Plyos to ensure that the guards at the dacha didn't see their chutes. Surprise was critical. Their chances of success would be drastically reduced, practically eliminated, if Shcherbatov's men knew that they were coming. A high-altitude, low-opening jump was the best way of ensuring stealthy infil; they would exit the aircraft while it was still plenty high, open the main chute after a long free fall and then glide the canopy all the way to the target. They would land twenty kilometres away from the jump point.

Milton did his last-minute checks and, satisfied, walked to the ramp.

The jumpmaster pointed out the back.

Number Two jumped and then, a moment later, so did Six, Eight and Nine. Milton was left with Callan at the lip of the ramp, both of them looking down at the ground, mantled with ice, thousands of feet below.

'After you,' Callan shouted, making an extravagant sweeping gesture with his right arm.

Milton nodded, not willing to engage him, and dived off the ramp.

He fell for seventy-five seconds at terminal velocity, following the line of dots below him. He had an altimeter strapped to his wrist, but he had jumped hundreds of times before and didn't need it. He knew the time to open the canopy and, as he reached the right moment, he yanked the handle and watched the main chute billow out overhead. His speed sheared to twenty miles an hour and his body pulled five Gs.

The noise of the airplane's engines and the whistling rush of the wind disappeared and everything was silent. The stars spread out above him, diamonds sprinkled over the vault of night. Milton tugged the straps to make himself a little more comfortable and aligned himself with the others, further along in the descent, their black canopies swooping out like wings above them as they stacked for landing.

Milton closed his eyes for a moment and composed himself. The only sounds were the chute snapping overhead and his breathing, deep and easy. Milton opened his eyes again and, with his right hand, snapped the night-vision optics down from the rail system that was attached to the side of his helmet. The landscape below was suddenly bathed in a wash of eerie green. It looked peaceful and, more importantly, empty. He touched the controls and selected infrared; he saw a couple of heat sources but satisfied himself that they were animals. A couple of elk, drinking at a stream, about to get a surprise.

The agents below swooped in, landed twenty feet from the nearest snowmobile and immediately began to stow their chutes. Milton dropped to twenty feet, flared the parachute and landed on his feet. He unhooked his harness, worked it over his shoulders and away. He heard the flapping of Callan's canopy as he circled overhead, dropping suddenly and landing alongside with the same practiced ease that comes of repetition.

Spenser and Underwood used retractable shovels to excavate a narrow trench and they each stuffed their canopies inside, covering them up again with the snow until the only sign that they had been there was the disturbed drift.

That would be righted soon enough.

As Milton crunched across to the snowmobile, a snowflake landed on his nose. Thirty seconds later and a blizzard had started.

47

Milton looked at the others with wary caution. They were checking their weapons for damage from the jump, ensuring for a final time that magazines were full and that their complement of grenades and blasting charges had not fallen from their pockets or been detached from the velcro holding straps.

They worked quickly and in silence, completely professional. Each one of them was lethally dangerous. Trust was impossible, and yet, each of them had to cover the back of the others if the mission was to be a success. Milton had thought about whether to ask for more bodies. He had even considered asking for every operational member of the Group, but he had decided that they stood a better chance with a smaller, more agile unit. The six of them would be a match for twice as many guards, but success depended upon the element of surprise and ruthless execution of the plan. There were variables: perhaps Shcherbatov had increased the security, maybe Pope had been moved after all. But there was nothing that could be done about things that were out of his control.

Their weapons had been strapped to the chassis of the snowmobiles. Milton undid the bindings around his M4 and checked the carbine and the M320 grenade launcher that was slung beneath it. Both had survived the descent without damage. He removed the magazine and then pushed it back again. The carbine was shorter than a full-length rifle and better suited to close-quarters combat. It was a good gun but dependent upon regular cleaning; Milton had taken it to bits and reassembled it after he had finished with his handgun. He had his Sig in a shoulder holster, four magazines for the M4 in a mag pouch, two hundred rounds of ammunition, six fragmentation grenades, two blasting charges and a Benchmade Infidel knife.

There were three snowmobiles and six of them. Milton straddled the nearest snowmobile and started the engine. The headlamp flicked on, a beam of golden light filled with fat flakes of snow. Hammond crunched through the crust of snow and rode pillion. The others got onto their own vehicles, two to each machine. The other two engines started without issue. Milton took off the goggles, shoved them into his Bergen and replaced them with a pair of Oakley Ballistics.

'One, Group,' Milton announced into the radio. 'Comms check.'

'This is Eight. Comms check affirmative.'

'Two, affirmative.'

'Six, loud and clear.'

'Nine, check is good.'

'Ten, affirmative.'

Milton consulted his satnav. 'Twenty clicks,' he said. 'Couple of hours, provided the road is where it's supposed to be,'

'And that it's clear,' Hammond said.

'Don't worry about that. Ivan keeps his roads open, no matter what. It'll be clear.'

48

It took them a couple of hours to reach Plyos.

They hid the snowmobiles in the grounds of an empty dacha on the edge of the village and tracked the rest of the way on foot. The six of them were split into three teams: Alpha Team was Spenser and Underwood; Bravo Team was Milton and Callan; Charlie Team was Blake and Hammond. On Milton's signal, they dispersed to their prearranged attack points. Milton and Callan scaled the side of an empty barn that, from the gently sloping roof, offered a good view of Shcherbatov's dacha.

Milton watched as Alpha and Charlie Teams took their positions.

Spenser and Underwood ducked behind a parked car a hundred feet from the entrance to the dacha.

Blake and Hammond held position behind a low wall.

The roof was thick with snow and Milton sank down deep into it as he lay flat. Callan took position next to him, settling his M110 semi-auto sniper rifle on its bipod and taking aim through the scope. Below them and away to the east, Spenser was prone on the ground beneath an old Soviet-era Lada that was so buried beneath snow that it couldn't have been moved for weeks. He, too, had set up his rifle and was taking aim.

Milton swept the IR binoculars left and right, studying the dacha. He matched the compound's layout against the video from the overflight of a Russian TU-300 Korshun drone from earlier that afternoon and what he could remember from his brief visit earlier that week.

Everything was just as it should be.

It was encircled by high stone walls with a large decorative wooden gate guarding the entrance. Beyond that was a short drive through a thicket of trees. Two large buildings, the main residence and a smaller guest house, had been constructed inside with a neat and tidy courtyard between the two. A Russian army jeep was parked near to the residence. An armoured Tigr personnel transport was next to the jeep.

Milton focused on the heat traces from the guards.

'One, Group. Eyes on four tangos: two lookouts on the first floor, east and west third-floor balconies. Two foot patrols, one at the gates and another in the grounds.'

'*Two, One,*' Spenser responded. '*Guard dogs?*'

'Negative. I'm just getting those four. The others will be inside.'

'*Six, One. Can you see what they're carrying?*'

'AK-9s, AS-Vals,' Milton reported. 'They've got night-vision goggles. Can anyone make out an officer?'

No one could.

'No sergeant, either. If an officer is here, he's keeping warm inside.'

'*See the Tigr?*' Callan reported. '*Engine's cold, fresh snow on the roof, been there a while.*'

'Affirmative. Could come in useful. Can anyone see anything else? No roving patrols?'

The replies came back in the negative.

'One, Nine. Have you confirmed all phone and power and data lines are above ground?'

'*Confirmed,*' Underwood said. '*I'll cut them on command.*'

'All right then. We'll assume half a dozen inside . . .'

'*Unfair odds for them,*' Underwood said.

'But there's a chance that they've got a relief bivouac down in the village. We'll have to be quick and alive to avoid getting flanked.'

The mission had been constructed with a thirty-minute envelope in mind. Local Russian security forces and police would know that they were here soon enough and they didn't want to be in situ when they arrived. There would be no immunity for them if they were caught. They would be cut loose and left high and dry.

'*We know what we're doing, Milton,*' Spenser radioed back tersely.

Spenser was the ranking agent. Milton taking control must have rankled him.

Tough shit.

'One, Group. All units, safeties off, weapons tight.'

Milton held the glasses to his eyes and waited an extra second, just to be sure.

'Alpha, Bravo, Charlie. Status check, comms check, sound off. On my mark.'

He watched a moment longer, waiting for the guard on the facing balcony to turn his head away.

'Execute.'

Milton lay still and observed.

The opening of the assault was terrifying in its efficiency. Underwood cut the power to the compound and all of the lights were extinguished at once, plunging it into darkness. Just as the lights cut out, Spenser and Callan fired single shots from their suppressed rifles. Milton watched through the IR. The guards on the two balconies were both struck, one of them toppling over the balustrade and thudding into the deep drift beneath.

Hammond, who had crept from cover to cover until she was twenty feet from the gate, popped up and squeezed off two, short, silenced bursts. Another spray of tracer in the goggles. The guards who had been stationed at the street entrance were peppered and fell to the ground.

'One, Group. Weapons free, let's go and get Pope.'

49

'*Going explosive, main gate,*' Hammond said over the troop net.

Milton had stowed the binoculars, pulled down his goggles and switched to night vision. They had dismounted the building quickly and sprinted for the muster point at the dacha's gate. He could see Hammond, kneeling down at the wooden gates and slapping the explosive to the lock. Blake, Spenser, Underwood and Callan were arrayed behind her, pulling security, their weapons focused on the hole that she was about to create.

'*Fire in the hole.*'

Here we go.

Hammond hit the detonator and the blast buckled the gate right down the middle. Spenser was the first to attack it, kicking and yanking at the rent until it was wide enough for the others to pass through. Milton was the last to pass inside, turning his body so that his gear didn't snag against the sharp edges of the split wood.

Beyond the gate was the small courtyard.

The six of them communicated over the troop net as they split up into their assigned roles. Milton and Callan's first target was to clear the guest house. It was secured by a set of metal double doors with a glass window slit across the top; a window to the right had bars across the glass. There was no light in the windows and that made Milton nervous. The Russians would definitely have heard them breach the gate, which meant that anyone here had either moved to the main building or they were inside, waiting in ambush.

Callan let him go first. It wasn't because of cowardice; Milton was quite sure that a psychopath like Callan was not prey to something as mundane as fear. He wanted Milton in front of him so that he could keep an eye on him and so, perhaps, that he could put a bullet into his back once they had achieved their objective. But there was no time to worry about that now.

Milton tried the handle. It was locked. He unlatched the small sledgehammer from the back of his kit and struck the lock with a hard downward swipe. The hammer clashed into the knob, but it was strong and didn't break. He tried again with no more luck.

'One, Group,' he radioed. 'Going explosive.'

He stepped back, reaching around again but this time for a breaching charge. He peeled the adhesive backing from the charge and was on one knee, ready to place it, when the doors were suddenly flung open. A guard was above him, firing out in a wild burst. Milton rolled to the side, the rounds passing above his head. He was fortunate that he was already down or they would have cut him in half. He saw movement inside, a figure revealed as his goggles adapted to the deeper darkness inside the room. He brought up the M4 and squeezed off a tight volley, catching the man diagonally across his body and dropping him to the ground.

A second man appeared at the back of the room. Callan fired, the rounds whistling above Milton's head and stitching a dozen bullets into his head and torso.

'Shots fired,' Callan reported. 'Tangos down.'

The door had swung backwards again, half closing. Milton got up and approached it cautiously, nudging it open with the barrel of his rifle. He heard a voice calling out. He tightened the grip on his weapon. He saw a figure in the green glow of his night-vision goggles. It was a woman. He held his breath, nudging the M4 around until the infrared laser sight rested on her head. She was holding something. Milton held the laser sight steady. He felt the give of the trigger beneath his index finger. She stepped forward; Milton gave the trigger a little more pressure; she changed her stance, revealing a baby in her arms.

'Stay where you are,' he said in Russian.

'Don't shoot.'

Callan stepped up behind him and a second laser sight flashed across the woman's face.

Milton held up a hand to hold him back.

'Who are you?'

'Just nanny.'

Two additional children appeared behind her, hiding behind the black fabric of her dress.

'Come forward,' Milton called out.

He kept the sight steady on her forehead as she did as she was told, the children holding onto her legs.

'You killed them,' the woman said. 'They are dead.'

'Who are they?'

'Guards. The colonel's men.'

Milton glanced beyond her. The night vision revealed a pair of feet in the doorway of the room, pointing up to the ceiling. Callan aimed down and fired two shots into the body, then aimed at the second body and repeated the trick.

'One, Group. Guest house secure,' Milton reported. He cracked a ChemLight and dropped it at the guest house's front door to indicate the building was safe. 'Is the colonel here?'

'I believe,' she said.

'And the Englishman who was here a few days ago?'

'Yes,' she said. 'Definitely. Guards for him.'

'Where? The basement?'

'No. In bedroom. Third floor. He is sick.'

'Stay here,' Milton said. 'Don't come out, not for anyone. We'll be gone in ten minutes.'

Milton and Callan hurried across the courtyard.

'One, Group,' he spoke into the throat mike. 'Pope is not in the basement. They may have moved him to a third-floor bedroom.'

'Two, One,' Spenser said. *'Copy that. We're splitting.'*

Milton slid behind a low wall and brought his rifle up to bear on the dacha. There were two exterior doors, north and south, and they had divided the team so that they could control both. Milton was not able to say for sure whether there was a corridor connecting the two doors. If there was, detonating charges on both doors at the same time could lead to explosive overpressure, which would be unpredictable and dangerous. They had decided that Spenser and Underwood would attack the north door first and then Callan and Milton would breach the south. Blake and Underwood would retreat to the main gate for surveillance and crowd control and, if they needed it, reinforcement.

Callan prepared his charge, slapping it against the door and pulling back to wait for the order to blow it. Milton held his position, his laser showing green through his night vision as it danced across the wall of the building.

Spenser detonated the charge on the door on the other side of the building. Milton heard shots being fired: it was a close, controlled burst, from a weapon fitted with a suppressor. Likely an M4. There was a pause and then return fire, unsuppressed, the ragged *chack chack chack* of Russian AN-94s.

'*Heavy resistance*,' Spenser reported in a calm voice, bullets ricocheting nearby. '*Five or six soldiers, all behind cover. This isn't going to be easy.*'

'One, Alpha. Get well back. We'll blow the door from this side. Ten will attack from behind them. Use smoke. Copy?'

'*Copy. What about you?*'

'I'm going to go up.'

Milton heard suppressed fire across the radio. '*Copy, One. We're out of the way.*'

He turned to Callan. 'Initiate.'

Callan detonated the breaching charge. The rolling boom echoed around the courtyard and the door blew inwards. It fell so that it was blocking their path inside and, with Callan covering him, Milton went forwards and yanked it until he had moved it out of the way. The blast had knocked a soldier backwards, the pressure slamming him into the wall. He was knocked out cold. Callan aimed and fired two shots into his head. Milton watched with a mixture of horror and appreciation; he was utterly ruthless.

'Successful breach.'

Callan took two smoke grenades from his bandolier, popped them and tossed them down the corridor to the room in which the Russians had made their stand. Alpha Team had already thrown their grenades and the room was quickly filling with dense, impenetrable smoke. Milton doubted that the Russians would have been equipped with IR goggles. He heard the rattle of automatic fire, some suppressed, most not. The Russians were firing at shadows. Callan, Spenser and Hammond were picking off their targets carefully and efficiently

Like shooting fish in a barrel.

50

Milton put the noise of the firefight behind him as he started clearing up the stairs.

There were no lights and it was suspiciously devoid of activity. He took a right turn and made his way slowly up. The stairs were tiled, and a little slippery, and he moved with exaggerated care. Each step was set at a ninety-degree angle to the landing and half-landing above, with the result that it would have been very simple to prepare an ambush; anyone with an automatic weapon would be able to unleash a volley as soon as he made the landing, holding him and anyone else behind him in place. And they could not afford delay.

He reached the first floor. No lights had been lit. There were three bedrooms, including the ones in which Milton and Anna had slept. The bedrooms were empty.

There was a long rattle of gunfire below.

'One, Group. Report.'

'*Three down*,' Spenser said. '*Two, maybe three left. They're dug in.*'

'Copy that. First floor clear. Ascending to second.'

Milton turned the corner onto the second-floor landing. There was a narrow hallway, featureless and sparse, with a darkened archway at the end that should, if his understanding of the drone intel was correct, open onto a terrace running along the south side of the building. The corridor had four doors: the first two were near to where Milton was standing and the others towards the archway. Milton nudged his goggles so that they were more comfortably pressed against his eyes and made his way carefully down the hall, stopping at the first door before opening it with the point of his weapon and clearing inside. He opened the door to the adjacent room and cleared that, too. He continued along the corridor, clearing the remaining two rooms. All empty.

He moved towards the stairs.

He heard footsteps.

He saw a flash of movement just above and fired, his suppressed M4 announcing contact with a *BUP BUP BUP*. Moments later, a bloodied body, dressed in Russian army fatigues, slid down the stairs, flipped over onto its back and came to a stop. Milton put another two rounds into the man's head. Blood slicked down the tile treads of the stairs like the glistening path of a snail.

'Shots fired,' Milton reported. 'Tango down.'

Another one. Was that it?

The troop net buzzed with Blake's voice. *'Six, Group. We're outside the main gate. We've got activity.'*

'Two, Six. How bad?'

'Maybe a dozen coming our way. Lights on in a few houses.'

'Keep them back,' Spenser said. *'Two, One. Update, please.'*

Milton spoke, whispering into his mike: 'Going to third floor. Proceeding now.'

There couldn't be much further to climb. The stairwell was dark, no lights anywhere, but Milton's goggles gave him a good enough view. It had grown narrow and he moved carefully and diligently, taking no chances. He looked and listened for signs of movement, the sound of a round being chambered, anything; he got nothing. He was put in mind of the countless times he had been through the Killing House during SAS Selection all those years ago: a twenty-mile run so that they were exhausted and then a smoke-filled series of rooms, cut-out terrorists popping out from cover, live rounds fired into the cut-outs, and do it all again. That had been hard, and Milton had often resented it, but not now.

He reached the top of the stairs and turned the corner, onto the landing. His palms and fingers were slicked with sweat and he wiped his right hand against his combat trousers so that he had a better feel of the trigger.

The landing was short, a waist-high balustrade looking down onto the final flight of stairs, leading into a constricted hallway. There was a door at the end that led onto the balcony; he could see a narrow sliver of midnight sky through the slit of window, a sprinkling of stars, a quarter of the moon.

The shooting downstairs had stopped.

'Two, Group. Seven tangos down. Ground floor clear.'

Halfway along the corridor were two doors, one on each side. Milton proceeded slowly down the corridor, his gun up.

51

A switch was flicked and light crashed into Milton's night vision, blinding him, and then he was grabbed by the lapels and hauled into one of the rooms, the M4 pressed impotently up against his chest.

He was still blind as someone yanked him around and slammed him hard against the wall, forcing the rifle from his grip and sending it clattering to the floor. He was punched in the gut once and then twice and then a third time, and then a fourth blow dinged him on the point of his chin and the room dimmed for a moment.

He was bounced off the wall again and, when he stumbled back in the other direction, a garotte looped over his head and it was only instinct that saw him stab his right hand inside the noose to stop it closing around his throat. His assailant grunted as he yanked the wire tight; Milton staggered back into his body and felt slabs of muscle. The wire bit into the soft flesh of his hand as he stamped down with the heel of his boot, raking the shin of the man behind him. The man's grip did not falter and so Milton brought both legs up and kicked off the wall, sending both of them stumbling across the room like drunks. They hit a bed, bouncing off the mattress onto the floor beyond.

He swept his arm upwards, knocking the goggles from his face. There was blood on his wrist from where the wire had cut into his flesh.

The big soldier who had surprised him was already up. He had short cropped hair, hate-filled eyes, his shoulders and arms heavy with muscle.

Milton recognised him: it was Vladimir, the driver of the car that had brought him to Plyos with Anna.

Vladimir shone a smile that was full of bad intentions, reaching down and unsheathing a knife from the scabbard on his belt. He brought it up, the bright light shivering down the serrated edge, and passed it between both hands as he prowled towards Milton. Milton had no time to go for his pistol as Vladimir swung the knife into his ribs; Milton swept his right arm around to block the swipe, their wrists clashing. Vladimir jabbed and Milton swung to the side, then he slashed down and the blade sliced through the fabric of his shirt and opened up a six-inch gash on his forearm. Jags of pain scorched up from the wound.

The Russian changed tactics and charged him, driving him backwards again. Milton tripped on the edge of a rug and they fell, Milton underneath him, pressed down by the bigger man's weight. He smelt the sharp tang of vodka and sweat. Vladimir pinioned Milton's left hand with his right and, the knife in his left hand, pushed down. The knife started above his nose, close enough for him to see his own eye reflected in the steel, and then it jerked downwards, the point catching on the skin above his jawline and scratching a bloody furrow as it tracked down towards his throat.

Milton had his weaker left hand around Vladimir's wrist, but all he could do was slow the progress.

'*Blyadischa*,' Vladimir growled through his grunts of exertion.

The point of the knife drew blood as it pressed down on Milton's throat, the first few millimetres sinking into his flesh.

Milton worked his right leg free and drove his knee into the Russian's crotch. Vladimir's mouth gaped open and he released Milton's right hand and then Milton seized his chance, flashing down to the scabbard on his thigh and tearing out his own knife. He drew back his wrist so that the tip pointed upwards and punched it into Vladimir's chest. The strength drained out of the man immediately. Milton locked his hand around the hilt of the Benchmade, twisted it and thrust it up into his heart.

He pushed the big man off him.

He saw movement in the doorway.

His right hand went to his shoulder holster, bringing out the Sig. He rolled onto his stomach and aimed in a single, fluid motion.

Pascha Shcherbatov was stooping for the M4 he had dropped.

'Don't,' Milton said, his breath still ragged.

Shcherbatov stood. And raised his hands.

'I am unarmed. I surrender.'

Milton got up. Blood was running freely from the cut on the side of his hand and after he dabbed his fingers against his throat they were stained red. His jacket was tacky with the Russian's blood. He wiped the gore from his hand against his trousers and took a step towards the colonel.

'Hands on your head,' Milton ordered.

Shcherbatov did as he was told, lacing his fingers and resting his hands on his head.

Milton indicated with the gun and Shcherbatov stepped away from the M4, heading back into the corridor. Milton gestured that he should keep going and he went back into the room adjacent to the one where Vladimir had hidden from him.

It was dark. Milton brought the goggles back down again.

Ahead of him, against the sloping wall, was a narrow bed. There was someone on the bed.

'Very good, Captain Milton. I am impressed.'

He activated the torch attached to his helmet rails and a sharp, bright beam of white light trained onto Shcherbatov's face. He winced, a hand automatically coming down to shield his eyes.

'On your head!'

Shcherbatov replaced his hand and looked away.

'Anyone else up here?'

'No.'

'Just Vladimir?'

'That is right.'

Milton turned the lights onto the bed. Pope was laid out there. He looked worse than when Milton had seen him before. He was unshaven, with thick curls of beard, brown streaked with grey. His eyes were rheumy and uncertain and there were fresh bruises on his face.

'I did not expect this,' Shcherbatov said. 'It is Control's doing?'

'No. All my own work, I'm afraid.'

'How many of you?'

'Six.'

Shcherbatov looked surprised. 'An armed incursion onto Russian soil? That is a dangerous precedent for a little thing such as this.'

'Don't worry,' Milton said. 'We had help.'

'My comrades in Red Square, I presume?'

'What can I say? Turns out you're not a very popular fellow.'

Milton turned the lights back onto Shcherbatov's face and he squinted into them again. He laughed. 'Then my congratulations, Captain. You have outmanoeuvred me.'

'Pope,' Milton called out. 'Wake up.'

'Do not concern yourself. He has been well treated.'

'Is that right?'

'He has pneumonia. A doctor has been attending to him. He is not in danger.'

'Pope.'

'What will happen now, Captain Milton? You will finish the job you failed to do when we first met?'

'*Pope.*'

'I am not afraid of death.'

Milton had thought long and hard during the flight to Kubinka. Shcherbatov was not his enemy, not really, despite what he had done to Pope. The man wanted revenge for what had happened to Semenko and using him was his means to that end; that, Milton concluded, was reasonable. Milton was similarly inclined. They had both been burned by Control. His thoughts ran back to an innocent man, gunned down in cold blood in East London. He thought of all the men and women he had been sent to kill in the name of the state. He thought of the doubts that he now harboured about those jobs, about how many of them had been legitimate targets, deserving of the fate that he had dealt them. Really, how many? Two-thirds? Half? His doubts would never be answered as long as Control was in place at the head of Group Fifteen. But things might be different if he was removed.

That was the big picture; but it also served both him and Beatrix very well to leave Control with a problem that he would not be able to solve.

Shcherbatov's arms were spread. 'Please, Captain. You must do what you must.'

'I'm not going to shoot you, Colonel. I'm going to give you what you want.'

He tore open his thigh pocket and was reaching his fingers down into it when he heard footsteps behind him. His hand stopped as he half-turned, the beams of light raking across the wall towards the darkness of the doorway, just in time to see the muzzle flashes from Callan's suppressed M4.

He turned back into the room.

Shcherbatov was on the floor. Callan had shot him cleanly in the head. Three rounds. There was blood and brain matter around the entry wound. He was still moving a little, the last spasms that would precede a certain death, but Callan trained his laser on the old man's chest and fired two more rounds into him to hasten him towards his exit. The body spasmed again and then fell still.

'*Ten, Group. Last man down.*'

Milton turned to him, his fists clenched. 'What are you doing?'

'We had orders, Milton. Everyone here is to be eliminated. No witnesses.'

'Those weren't *my* orders.'

Callan was impassive. 'You don't work for us any more. I don't take my orders from you.'

Milton surreptitiously sealed the pocket again, leaving the drives where they were.

'*Six, Group,*' Blake reported over the radio. '*Hurry, please. There's more of them on the way out here.*'

'Bring him,' Callan said, indicating Pope with the muzzle of his M4.

Milton knew that the terrain was shifting beneath him.

He pulled his CamelBak hose from his kit and held it in front of Pope's chapped lips.

'John?' he said, his voice weak.

'You've got to get up, Pope.'

'We need to move now,' Blake said. 'I can hear police.'

Spenser's voice was tense. '*Ten, report.*'

'*Ten, Group,*' Callan said. '*Third floor secure.*'

'*Two, Ten. Copy that. Mission status?*'

'*Affirmative, Ten. SNOW is down.*'

52

Milton and Callan helped Pope down the stairs. He was barely able to support himself. They reached the ground floor and then the courtyard. He clasped his fingers around Pope's belt for a better grip as they picked him up and hurried towards the outside gate.

There were lights on in most of the nearby dachas; the residents had been awakened by the explosions and the gunfire. Milton could see the silhouettes of locals in their windows and perhaps two dozen had come outside and were climbing up the hill towards them. They were keeping a cautious distance, wary of the soldiers, but some of the more intrepid ones were only fifty feet away. Blake could speak fluent Russian and he bellowed out for them to go back inside. They didn't, but they didn't advance any further. It was a temporary stalemate, but Milton knew that eventually their curiosity would win out. There was also the question of footage of the raid finding its way online; he could see the glow of several smartphones held aloft to record the action. It would be on YouTube before they had crossed the town limits.

They carried Pope onwards. 'He won't be able to travel on the snowmobiles,' Milton said.

'You don't need to worry about that,' Spenser replied.

'What do you mean?'

Callan released his grip on Pope and stepped away. Milton had to bear the weight alone.

Callan raised his handgun and aimed it at Milton's head. 'On your knees,' he said.

Milton looked at Callan and then at the others. None of them looked surprised. Hammond and Spenser had stepped back a little, their hands resting on their automatic weapons, standing ready to provide support should it be necessary. Blake and Underwood had one eye on the crowd outside the wrecked gate and another on Milton. There was his confirmation, then: they were all in on it. It had always been part of the plan. Control was going to call his bluff after all. Bravo.

'Get it over with,' Spenser said to Callan. 'You wanted to do it, so do it.'

'Callan.' It was Pope; his voice was quiet and hoarse. Milton turned to look and saw that he had managed to raise his bruised face. 'What are you doing?'

'Control's orders,' Callan said, his gun arm unwavering. He was only six feet from Milton; it would have been impossible for an amateur to miss from that range, and Callan was not an amateur.

'What orders?' Pope said.

'He needs to be gone.'

'Take him into custody. You don't need to shoot him.'

'Be quiet,' Spenser snapped.

Underwood approached from behind and drove his boot into the back of Milton's knees. His legs folded and he fell forward, bracing with his left arm. Pope fell down with him, Milton's looped right arm preventing him from falling face first into the snow.

Milton felt calm. He had faced the prospect of death for most of his adult life and he was accustomed to it. It was a possibility that he had accepted; the long-term prognosis for agents working for Control was not good. Milton did not know the average, but he did know that plenty of men and women had been killed in duty in the time he had been in the Group. He had managed to avoid the same fate thanks to a combination of careful planning, decisive execution and good fortune, but that was never going to work forever. Luck always ran out. And, as he knelt there in the snow and the muck, he realised that he was tired of running. Control would never stop. He was relentless. Maybe it was better to just accept the inevitable.

'It's all right,' he said. 'Do what you have to do.'

He closed his eyes. The snow had quickly chilled the muscles in his calves and thighs and it was working up his spine. He breathed in and out and thought about the last six months: the long trek through South America, the time he had spent in San Francisco. Saving Caterina Morena. Meeting Eva. He had helped people. His account was far from being settled. It was still soaked in the blood that he had spilled, but he had started to make recompense.

It was not his fault that he had not been able to do more; he had simply run out of time.

'Callan . . .' Pope was protesting weakly.

'It has to be done.'

'Of course it doesn't.' The anger put a little of the steel that Milton remembered back into his voice.

'Enough, Pope,' Spenser spat.

Milton opened his eyes. Callan had taken a step away from him: pitilessly professional, sizing up the shot.

Pope was on his hands and knees, struggling to push himself upright.

Spenser intercepted him and kicked his arms away. 'You too, I'm afraid. Control doubts your loyalty. And you've already seen too much.'

Milton saw the satisfaction in Callan's handsome, cruel face as he racked the slide to cock the hammer, chambering the top round in the magazine. He had seen it before, in a church hall in the East End of London. Callan was a killer, pure and simple. Each of Milton's kills had scoured away a little more of the humanity that was left in his soul. But Callan was different: he found pleasure every time he pulled the trigger or used his knife or his garotte. He took pleasure in his job. In that sense, he was the perfect agent. No wonder he was Control's favourite new creature. He would go far.

Callan straightened his arm and aimed at Milton's head. Milton knew with certainty that there would be no successful appeal to his better nature.

He closed his eyes again and waited.

He heard the crunch of snow.

The shot didn't come.

Milton paused, holding his breath, wondering why he could still feel the cold working its way up between his shoulder blades, feel the rough texture on the inside of his gloves, the cold breath of winter on the patches of bare skin around his eyes and mouth.

He opened his eyes.

Callan wasn't there any more.

Milton rubbed the snow from his eyes. It looked as if a patch of the deep white drift at the side of the drive had detached and risen up. Snow and ice fell away, revealing the figure of a woman dressed in a makeshift ghillie suit. She was twenty feet away. He saw a parka with a mesh across the opening and shaggy threads sewn across it in horizontal lines to break up its outline, similarly adorned waterproof trousers and chunky boots. Her face was visible within the loop of the fur-trimmed hood.

Beatrix Rose.

She had two throwing knives, one in each hand.

Callan had fallen backwards and now he was facing straight up. Her first knife was buried in his throat. The knife was made of a single piece of steel. His carotid artery was severed and his still beating heart spent its terminal beats spraying aortal red blood across the dirty snow.

Milton's head snapped around just as Beatrix flicked out her right arm and sent her second knife on its way.

Blake's padded jacket seemed to absorb the knife, the blade disappearing into his gut, the impact and the surprise sending him staggering backwards, his hands clutching at the grip.

Spenser got a shot off, but the bullet went wide, ricocheting off the wall of the dacha.

Milton crawled across the gritty snow, pressed right down into it, until he reached Callan's body. He still had his Sig in his hand; Milton took it.

Hammond raised her rifle and fired an unaimed spray towards Beatrix. The bullets peppered the trees and the ground behind her, a dozen little explosions of snow jagging backwards. Beatrix ducked behind a tree, out of sight.

Hammond wasn't looking at Milton. He shot her in the right temple, her head jerking hard to the left as she fell to the ground.

Underwood saw him shoot and brought up his rifle, but Milton was quicker with the Sig and put two shots into his gut.

Spenser was last man standing. He turned and started to run, but Beatrix's left arm flicked out again and a third knife caught him in the thigh. His leg went out from beneath him and he collapsed sideways into a drift of snow. He scrabbled around so that he was facing back towards them.

Milton aimed at him with the pistol. 'Drop it!'

Spenser flung his weapon aside and raised his hands. 'Don't shoot,' he called out.

Beatrix came out from behind the tree and stalked through the drift towards him.

'On your knees,' Milton yelled back. 'Hands on your head.'

'My leg,' he said. 'I can't . . . my leg . . .'

It was moot: Milton might have been clement, but Beatrix was not so inclined. She reached down to the bandolier that was hidden beneath the ragged strands of the ghillie suit, a leather strap that stretched diagonally across her chest, with half a dozen sheathes spaced across it, and took out another knife. She knelt down in the snow and spoke to Spenser quietly; Milton couldn't make the words out. He protested. She ignored him, stepped around, slid the fingers of her left hand into his hair and yanked back, exposing his neck. She drew the knife across his larynx, opening his throat, the razor-sharp blade severing his trachea. His fingers clutched at the gruesome rent, helplessly trying to close it even as it gaped open and closed with the frantic up and down of his head. His hands slicked red, his body toppled backwards, hinging at the waist, his torso thudding back into the drift, the abundant blood drenching the snow a bright crimson.

Jesus, Milton thought.

'Is that it?' Beatrix called out.

Milton hurried back to Pope and helped him up. 'Are you all right?'

'Who's that?'

Beatrix was over Spenser's body. She wiped the bloodied blade on his jacket and slid it back into its sheath.

'You don't know her,' Milton said.

'Who?'

'Her name is Beatrix Rose. She used to be Number One.'

53

Milton hauled Pope into the back of the Tigr. It was an All Terrain Armoured Transport, much like an American Hummer. The benches behind the driver's and passenger's seats had been cleared from the interior and Milton pulled Pope all the way inside, reaching back to close the rear door. Beatrix had climbed into the front and turned over the big turbocharged diesel. The locals were up at the gate and the blue and red lights of a police car flashed against the sides of the buildings down the hill.

They had to get away.

'Go, go, go,' he shouted.

The Tigr lurched forwards, the tyres slipping until they found purchase and then slinging them ahead. Beatrix aimed down the hill that led away from the dacha, hitting the brakes at the bottom and swinging them around to the left and the road that would lead to Privolzhsk.

The police car came around the corner and followed after them. It was faster and, provided the road stayed clear up ahead, it would very quickly overhaul them. Milton held onto the side as he glanced back through the windows: it was a hundred feet behind them and closing fast.

'Milton!' Beatrix yelled. 'You need to do something about that car.'

Milton unlocked the rear doors and kicked them open. The blue and white painted car was fifty yards behind them now, close enough for Milton to see the driver and his passenger. He waited until they had passed onto a smooth section of road and, fixing his left hand around a stanchion, aimed his Sig with his right. The first shot struck the ground three feet in front of the car, throwing up a small cloud of grit and ice. Milton had not intended to hit the car, just warn the driver, but it did not have the desired effect: the passenger leant out and fired three shots with his own semi-automatic. The third caught the nearside mirror, shattering it.

Fair enough.

Thirty feet.

Milton extended his arm and aimed again, absorbing the recoil in his shoulder for a smoother shot. The bullet found its mark, slicing into the front-right tyre and shredding it so that it flapped off the wheel. The car swerved out of control, the driver braking hard and bleeding off most of the speed before the car spun across a sheet of ice and thumped into a deep drift that had been ploughed to the side of the road.

'Put your foot down.'

Milton grabbed hold of Pope's jacket to hold him in place as the Tigr bumped and bounced over the uneven road, ploughing through the fresh drifts that had not yet been cleared.

'How far is it?' Beatrix called back.

'Sixteen clicks,' Milton reported.

'So, say thirty minutes.'

'Come on, Beatrix, we've got no time. Pope needs medivac now. We need to be faster.'

Beatrix clunked the Tigr into fifth gear. She stamped on the accelerator and they lurched forwards.

'All right,' she said. 'Let's say twenty.'

Milton switched radio frequencies and brought the mike up so that it was pressed against his throat again. 'Any station, any station. This is Blackjack Actual in the clear. Radio check in the blind, over.'

There was a moment of silence, adorned by static, and then an accented Russian voice replied: *'This is Overlord. We have you five-by-five. Phase line Echo secure. State your position, over.'*

Milton looked out of the window and did his best to guess. 'Two clicks south of Plyos. Heading for exfil point. ETA twenty minutes, over.'

Milton could hear the sound of a big engine in the background. The speaker had to raise his voice to be heard. *'Acknowledged, Blackjack. What is the sit-rep in Plyos?'*

'Success.'

'The target?'

'Affirmative, Overlord.'

'Acknowledged, Blackjack. Make your way to exfil. We'll be there. Over and out.'

Pope coughed, a tearing sound that came from deep inside his lungs. He reached up for Milton's elbow. 'John,' he said, his voice a ragged whisper.

Milton leant down nearer to his face. 'Don't talk. We're getting you out.'

54

The Kamov Ka-60 had been airborne for some time already and it had been forced to circle the exfil point for twenty minutes.

Beatrix slalomed the Tigr through the deep snow at the side of the road, the Tigr decelerating sharply, and cut across the wide field to the clear space that Milton had indicated. He opened the door and dropped down, taking four ChemLights from his Bergen, cracking them alight and tossing them out to form the corners of a wide rectangle. The chopper's engines roared as it descended, the pilot flaring the nose and the vicious wash kicking up thick eddies of snow, blowing away the fresh fall to reveal the icy permafrost beneath.

Milton and Beatrix went around to the back of the Tigr and helped Pope down. They draped his arms across their shoulders and stumbled towards the Kamov, the toes of their boots catching against the ridges of snow and his carving long troughs behind him. There were two crew onboard, and the second man went back into the cabin and opened the door for them. Beatrix reached the chopper and vaulted up. Milton helped Pope inside, boosted him forwards and Beatrix hauled him the rest of the way. Milton vaulted up himself.

'Where are rest of your team?' the crewman called out.

'Didn't make it,' Milton said.

Milton was no pilot, but even he could tell from the anxiety in the open cockpit that the crew were concerned that they would have enough juice to make it back to Kubinka.

Nothing he could do about that.

He spun his finger in the air, the signal to take off. 'Let's get out of here.'

He sat with his back against the fuselage. He took off his helmet and scrubbed his fingers through his sweaty, bedraggled hair, then swiped the sweat from his eyes. Pope was shivering and Beatrix found a blanket and draped it over him. The crewman shouted back that there was hot coffee in the vacuum flask in the pack fastened to one of the chairs. She took it, poured out a cup and held it to Pope's lips. He sipped at it. Beatrix looked over at Milton with concern. Pope was very sick and very weak.

Milton turned to the pilot. 'How long to Kubinka?'

'Forty-five minutes,' the man shouted back.

'Is that at top speed?'

'Top speed, maybe thirty-five, but fuel . . .'

'Do it,' Milton said. 'He needs a doctor.'

* * *

The lights of Kubinka airfield blinked brightly in the snowy night. The runway was delineated by converging horizontal lines and then, beyond, red and green vertical stripes that marked the runway edges and the centre line. They could see the Moscow suburbs away to starboard, the urban glow shining through the darkness like a golden mantle. The pilot radioed that they were on final approach, swung the Kamov into a sharp turn and then bled the height away. They were coming down on the runway itself, aiming for the darkened outline of the Hercules, its white landing lights refracting brightly against the wetness of the cleared asphalt beneath it.

The rotors eddied the flakes as their ride touched down and Milton was the first to disembark, bent low to manage the wash as he crossed to the RAF flight lieutenant who had flown the Hercules that had brought them in. He was standing with three Russian airmen. The Hercules was twenty feet away, the four big engines already rumbling and the propellors turning slowly.

'Welcome back, sir. Everything all right?'

'Everything is fine, Lieutenant.'

'Where are the others?'

'They're not coming back.'

'What happened?'

'They were ready for us,' he lied. 'Heavy resistance. The others didn't make it.'

'I'm sorry, sir.'

'We need a stretcher. Captain Pope is very weak.'

'Already sorted that out, sir. We'll bring it across.'

'And the doctor?'

'Over there, sir.' The flight lieutenant pointed to the medic who was running towards the Kamov.

'Are you ready to go?'

'We'll be on our way in five minutes. Don't see much point in hanging around, do you?'

'No, Lieutenant, I do not.'

'Get aboard then, sir. I'll make sure our man gets on in one piece.'

Milton paused. 'Got a smoke?'

He didn't, but one of the Russians nodded and offered Milton a packet of Java Zolotaya. Milton thanked him, took one and tried to hand the packet back; the Russian held up his hand and shook his head. Milton thanked him again. He put the cigarette to his lips and lit it.

The flight lieutenant led the Russians to the Kamov.

Beatrix stepped down and walked over to him.

'Thanks,' Milton said.

'I thought I was going to be late. The car *Mamotchka* gave me broke down in the middle of nowhere. I hitched the rest of the way.'

'You *hitched?*'

'Truck driver took pity on me. Probably thought his luck was in.'

She cocked an eyebrow in amusement. It wasn't difficult to imagine how quickly he would have been disabused of that idea.

They walked across the airstrip to the Hercules. The ramp was already lowered and they climbed aboard, knocking their boots against the hydraulic struts to clear the compacted snow away.

Milton watched her. 'You know Spenser was surrendering, don't you?'

'I know,' she said.

'I'm not being critical.'

'I wouldn't care if you were,' she said. 'He had it coming to him.'

'You had history?'

'We did.'

'He was one of the ones Control sent after you?'

'He took my daughter,' she said absently. 'I'd kill him twice if I could.'

'The score is settled, then.'

'With him, yes. Just five more now.'

Milton looked at her: there was steel in her face and fire in her eyes. He didn't press.

He finished his cigarette and threw it onto the runway outside. The Russians had Pope on a stretcher and they were bringing him across to them.

He took out the packet. 'These taste like shit. You want one?'

'Go on, then.'

He handed one to her and then gave her his lighter. She lit it, holding it between her lips as she took the pistol from its holster, secured the manual safety and then ejected the magazine. The action was completed easily and smoothly, with minimum effort. He knew she would have been able to strip and reassemble the gun when she was blindfolded, too. He was just the same. He remembered what she had been like when she had selected him from the other applicants who had been competing to join the Group: fierce and intimidating, and none of that edge had been dulled in her lost years. Her anger had become a crucible and she had submerged herself in that slow-burning, pitiless flame, until the emotion had been smelted out of her.

PART 7

LONDON

55

Control sat at the wide table and glared with undisguised disdain at the three men opposite him. It was a senior deputation: the Foreign Secretary, a particularly oleaginous politician called Gideon Coad of whom Control had always had a rather bleak opinion, together with the heads of MI5 and MI6. It was midnight and the meeting had been called as a matter of the greatest urgency. The evidence had been delivered earlier that day. It had arrived by email, from an anonymous account that had been accessed at an internet café in Hounslow. Agents had been sent to the café to question the owner, but he could not remember anything of the customer who had booked fifteen minutes at the machine from which the email had been sent. When they checked his security cameras, they found that they had been disabled. Whomever had sent the email, they had an interest in hiding their identity.

Control had not been given advance warning of the subject of the meeting, although, after the failure of any of the five agents to respond, it was not difficult to guess.

They had taken thirty minutes to run through the extensive evidence with which they had been presented. There were the pictures of Control with Alexandra Kyznetsov and the correspondence and financial details that had been culled from the flash drives. That, in itself, would have been enough to damn him, but they hadn't stopped there.

They had obtained *ex camera* search orders and collected his bank details for the last ten years. He was not foolish enough to have passed the money he had received from Kyznetsov, or the other people like her who had come afterwards, through accounts that could easily be traced. There were other accounts for that, ones in jurisdictions that did not so easily divulge their secrets, but even with those precautions in place, they had put questions to him that he had struggled to answer: how had he found the money to purchase his property outright, for example? He had paid for his Jaguar in cash. Where had that come from? The holidays, the extravagant purchases. They suggested that they exceeded his income. They accused him of living beyond his means.

Where was the money coming from?

Control knew that they had already reached their conclusion and that anything he said could only incriminate him further, and so he deflected them all with bluster. How did they find the *temerity* to question a man who had given so much to his country?

It didn't matter. He had already started to plan his next steps. He had already started, in truth, as soon as it became obvious that the mission to Plyos had failed. Forewarned was forearmed and he had always feared that this day would come, no matter how careful he had been. He had steps in place and, knowing that, he was able to brazen it out.

'Do you have anything you want to say?' Coad asked him.

'Just that I find it difficult to understand how you could accuse me of wrongdoing.'

'No one is accusing you of anything,' he corrected calmly. 'We're simply saying that there are some questions that need to be answered.'

'Semantics,' Control snorted derisively.

Coad held up his hands in a gesture of helplessness. 'We don't really have a choice in this, old man. We're going to have to suspend you until this can be cleared up. Shouldn't take longer than a month, I should think. I'm sure there's a perfectly good set of answers that will make this all go away. And, when we have them, you'll be back in post.'

Control got up. 'Is that all?'

'Stay in the country, all right?'

'Anything else?'

'No. That's all.'

He nodded curtly, collected his overcoat from the stand next to the door and made his way to the street outside.

*   *   *

He knew he didn't have long and so he drove straight to Waterloo. There was a large warehouse not far from the station that had been transformed into a secure storage facility, and Control had rented a space there for the past five years. He took a walk-on suitcase from the boot of the car, showed his driving licence at the desk and went through the doors into the warren of corridors that had been fashioned by hundreds of crates of varying sizes. The one he wanted was of medium size, big enough to stand erect but small enough that he could touch all four walls from the centre. He unlocked the door, stepped inside, and switched on the light. He closed the door behind him. There was just one item inside the room: a hundred-litre crate made of opaque plastic. He opened the lid and began to inventory the items inside.

Weapons first. He took out the Heckler & Koch MP7A1 machine pistol wrapped in oilcloth, followed by the sound suppressor. Beneath that were three thirty-round magazines and six boxes of ammunition. There was a FNP-45 .45 calibre double-action semi-automatic with one extra magazine.

He put the guns into the suitcase and went back to the crate.

There were six Tesco plastic bags, the heavy-duty ones that were supposed to last for life, and, inside, was thirty thousand pounds and ten thousand dollars, all in tens and fifties. A Ziplock freezer bag held French and German passports in different names and matching driver's licences. There was a wallet with a third driver's licence and a credit card in the name of Peter McGuigan that would allow him to access the Cayman account with two hundred thousand dollars in it. There was a packet of hair dye, a pair of spectacles with clear frames and a handheld GPS.

He packed the items into the suitcase, left the empty crate behind him, locked the door to the storage room and went back outside to his car. He put the suitcase into the boot and, before he closed the lid and after checking that he wasn't observed, he opened the case, withdrew the semi-automatic and covered it beneath his overcoat as he went around to the driver's side and got into the car.

*   *   *

It was a two-hour drive to the south coast from Waterloo. He drove carefully so as not to draw attention to himself, following the A23, M23, A23 again and then the A26 until he reached Lewes. He passed the Beachy Head Hotel and the sign for the Samaritans at the side of the road: 'Always There, Day or Night', the last appeal to those who were intent upon doing away with themselves. It was a beautiful spot, the exposed promontory whipped by the winds that blew in from the Channel. The white chalk cliffs were five hundred feet high here and the vertiginous drop to the spume-crested rocks below had claimed hundreds of lives; Control had read somewhere that it was the third most popular place for suicides in the world.

He parked the Jaguar in the car park, leaving the keys in the ignition, collected the suitcase from the boot, and wheeled it back to the bus stop that he had passed as he drove in. There was a telephone box next to it. He went inside and called the local minicab office that had left business cards wedged into the sides of the window.

The operator picked up after a dozen rings.

'I need a taxi.'

'Where are you, mate?'

'Beachy Head.'

'And where do you want to go?'

'Southampton Airport, please. Quick as you like.'

Control stood outside the telephone box and watched as the fiery rim of the sun slid above the edge of the cliff, the light flooding into the midnight blue of the sky. The dawn chorus greeted it noisily and a milk float rattled and chinked as the driver pulled in with his delivery.

Control drew his overcoat around him and breathed in a lungful of fresh, salty air. It looked like it was going to be a beautiful day.

56

Milton got off the underground at Heathrow Terminal Five. The platform was crowded with travellers, some with hand-held luggage, others hauling cases on wheels. He took his place on the escalator and rode it all the way to the first floor and the departure lounge. A travelator hurried the seemingly endless queue of travellers onwards: parents corralling boisterous children; business travellers with newspapers open before them; backpackers with grungy T-shirts and brightly coloured bracelets on their wrists. Milton waited in line. There was no sense in rushing; he wasn't in any kind of hurry.

The huge, cavernous shed opened out before him: hundreds of check-in desks, thousands of passengers. There was a Starbucks concession this side of security and Milton headed for it.

A man was sitting at one of the shiny metal tables. Milton sat down opposite him.

'Pope.'

'Milton.'

Pope's face still bore the evidence of his beating at the hands of Pascha Shcherbatov. His eyes were still bruised, but the vivid purple had faded away, to be replaced by a dull puce.

He shifted in his chair, better to accommodate the residual pain from the ribs that had been broken.

'How are you feeling?' Milton asked.

'I'm fine.'

'You don't look it.'

'But I look better than I did?'

'You look old.'

'We both look old, John. We *are* old.'

'Speak for yourself.'

Anna Kushchyenko walked towards them from Boots, carrying a small bottle of water. She stood at the table and offered Milton her hand; he took it.

'Captain Milton,' she said with cold formality.

'Anna. How are you?'

'I'm very well.'

The conversation was stilted; he had hurt her pride for the second time.

'Are you going to sit down?'

'I don't think so. My flight leaves soon.'

She was dressed in a business suit with a white shirt, similar to the outfit that she had been wearing when she had got him out of trouble in Texas. That seemed an awfully long time ago now.

She looked down at him: beautiful, frigid, haughty.

'I'm not going to say I'm sorry, Anna. It was business. It had to be done. But, for what it's worth, you are an excellent agent. You just need a little seasoning.'

She stiffened. 'I don't need your apology,' she said curtly, 'and I don't need your advice.'

'I'm sorry about the colonel. What happened to him wasn't what we planned.'

Anger flashed. 'No? What did you have planned?'

'I was going to give the flash drives to him.'

Did she believe him? It didn't look like it. She shook her head derisively, the curtain of red hair shifting across her shoulders. She collected her bottle of drink from the table. 'I should be going,' she said. 'Goodbye, Captain Milton.'

'Goodbye, Anna.'

'Perhaps we will see each other again.'

'Perhaps.'

57

Milton and Pope wandered across to the wide windows of the observation lounge. It was a dark night, the moon and stars hidden by a thick blanket of low cloud. The 747 liveried in the colours of Aeroflot lumbered down the runway, raised its front wheel from the tarmac and struggled into the air. Anna would be back in Moscow in four hours.

'Have we spoken to the Russians?' Milton asked.

'I believe so.'

'And?'

'They're not unhappy. As far as they're concerned, you did what you said you'd do.'

They strolled to a couple of empty seats and sat down.

'Here,' Pope said, proffering a new passport.

Milton flicked through the pages; they were clean, unstamped, virgin. There was something to be written there. Possibilities.

'Thanks.'

'Look at the last page.'

Milton did: the passport was in his own name, not an alias.

'You're in the clear, John. You are officially retired.'

'That's easy for you to say.'

'I'm serious. It's finished, John. You can do whatever you want to do.'

'You know that for a fact?'

'I do.'

'And does Control see it that way?'

'He isn't going to be a problem any more. Not for you, anyway.'

'They got rid of him?'

Pope paused, an awkward grimace on his face, and Milton connected the dots.

'Seriously? They took him out?'

'He's been given a file.'

'But?'

'But he can't be found. His car was found at Beachy Head last night. The keys were still in the ignition.'

'No way,' Milton said. 'He's faked it. He didn't jump. He's a cockroach, Pope. It's going to take more than that to get rid of him.'

Pope nodded his agreement. 'They've searched the rocks and they didn't find anything. We don't think he jumped either. He's running. I don't even want to think what they're going to find out when they dig into what he's been doing all this time. The number of files he passed down to us for actioning ... how many of those were people he wanted out of the way? I can deal with it if I know that the target deserves what's coming to them. If they were to cover for him, though, that's something else.'

'I've been thinking that, too.'

'Shcherbatov would have been pleased.'

'He would have said the job was only half done.'

'Yes, but we'll finish it. He can't run forever. We'll find him.'

Milton stopped, looking at his old friend. 'Hold on,' he said, a slow realisation dawning. 'Who's replacing Control?'

Pope shrugged.

'You?'

'They asked me yesterday.'

'And you said no.'

He smiled ruefully.

'You said *yes?* Don't be an idiot.'

'It's the only way they're ever going to get off your back.'

'You don't have to do that for me.'

'It's not just for you. I'm the same age as you. You think I want to be in the field for ever? I'm old and slow. I was sloppy last time. I got lucky.'

Milton protested. 'But you're not a politician. Get into private security. Go and be a consultant somewhere. Make some money. You think you can work with the government? They'll eat you up.'

'Ouch,' he said. 'A little more credit, please. It's in your interest to see me do well. I'm the one who's saying there's no point in chasing you halfway around the world anymore. I'm the one saying you're free to do whatever you want. I rescinded your file. That was the first thing I did.'

The two of them paused; Milton didn't know what to say. He knew that Pope was a superb agent, not as good as he had been, but *good*, and that having him ride a desk was a criminal waste of his talents. But, as his old friend smiled with patient affection at him, he realised that, maybe, his promotion had benefited from a little good sense. Pope was solid and dependable and, after the corruption and avarice that had latterly been exposed in his predecessor, those were not unhelpful qualities to have. He was strong-willed, the kind of man who would question his orders and, Milton thought, that too would be a useful trait.

'You're not going to congratulate me?'

'For accepting a poisoned chalice? You couldn't pay me to do that job.'

There was a moment of awkwardness between them. Pope slapped his hands on his knees, dispelling it. 'What are you going to do next?'

Milton thought about that. 'I don't know,' he said. 'If the Group isn't looking for me, I don't have to hide.'

'No,' Pope agreed. 'You can go wherever you like. You need money?'

'Does it look like I'm begging?'

'No. I think it looks like you're leaving with nothing.'

'What else do I need?' Milton shrugged.

'No luggage at all?'

'If I need something, I'll get it when I arrive. I've always travelled light.'

'You know where you're going?'

'I've made a habit of not telling people that,' he said, and then when Pope frowned at him, he added, 'Wherever seems right.'

'I can't persuade you to stay around?'

'There's nothing for me here.'

Milton really didn't know what he wanted to do or where he wanted to go. His plan was to walk into the departures lounge, look at the flights that were leaving in the next couple of hours, pick one, buy a ticket, and go.

'You want some advice? If it were me, I'd find somewhere I liked and I'd stay there a while. Put down some roots.'

'That's not me,' Milton said. 'I've been on the move for six months. I've got no ties. Don't think I want any.'

'You don't want a woman? Get a family?'

'Do I look like a family man? I'll leave that to you. I've never been cut out for it.'

And, he thought, *I've got too much that I need to do. Too much to make amends for.*

'All right, then,' Pope said. 'I'll leave you to it.'

He offered his hand and Milton took it.

'Thanks,' he said. 'You didn't have to do what you did. I won't forget it. If you need me, you know where I am. All right?'

Milton felt a moment of hesitation.

He looked up at the screen with two dozen destinations on it.

'Good luck,' Pope said.

'You too.'

Milton put the new passport in his hip pocket and walked towards the nearest ticket desk.

58

Pope had left his car in the short-stay car park. They had offered him a driver and a better car, but he wasn't interested in either; the old Control had been in post for so long that it felt like the time was right for a change in approach. He would do things his own modest way, and if that meant doing them quietly and without extravagance, then so be it. He could only be himself.

He unlocked the door and sat down. He was reaching for the engine start button when he was aware of someone in the car behind him.

'Easy.'

He felt a prickle of tension across his shoulder blades.

He knew who it was.

'Hello, Beatrix.'

He looked into the rear-view mirror: it was dark, but there was enough of a glow from the courtesy light to see her sallow face and long blonde hair. She was sitting back against the seat, unmoved and unconcerned, her cold blue eyes staring at him in the mirror. She was wearing a tight-fitting leather jacket.

'I needed to speak to you,' she said.

'You couldn't make an appointment?'

'I'd prefer it if we could keep it between us.'

The courtesy light faded out and Pope could only see her as a dark shadow. 'You don't have anything to hide from any more.'

'Old habits die hard.'

'No one is looking for you. Control has gone.'

'Yes,' she said. 'That's what I want to talk to you about.'

Pope rested his hands on the wheel. 'I'm sorry. I don't know where he is. No one knows. You have my word.'

'You understand why I want him?'

'Yes. What happened to your family. I know. Milton told me.'

'And you know I can't let that stand.'

'Yes, of course. I'd be the same.'

'So I need you to find him and give him to me.'

'I know I owe you. What you did for me will buy plenty of favours. But that's going to be very difficult to arrange.'

'Difficult but not impossible.'

'No. Not impossible.'

'I'm not expecting favours, Pope. I can pay my way.'

'With what?'

'I know you're replacing him.'

'How do you know that?'

'Never mind. You want to know how I see this? Control has left you a group of agents that you can't trust. He picked all of them and you don't know which ones were involved with him and which ones weren't. For all you know, they all were. That would be the safe assumption. Five of them are dead and you're out of the game. That leaves six. I don't know about you, but not being able to trust them wouldn't make me feel very safe. If you agree to work with me, I'll vet all of them for you: surveillance, background checks, whatever you need. All off the books. You and I would be the only ones who know.'

'And if we find any of them are crooked?'

'I'll take care of them.'

He knew what *that* meant.

'You need to know something else, too,' she said. 'I don't want to get our relationship off on the wrong foot, but I have the evidence to prove what Control did. Milton gave it to me. I sent it to the government. They have it just as they want it at the moment: Control is gone and you've taken his place with no fuss and no noise. Smooth and seamless. But it wouldn't take very much to rake over those coals again. I could easily send it all to a newspaper.'

'That sounds like a threat.'

'Depends how you take it,' she said. 'That's not what I want it to sound like.'

'What do you want it to sound like?'

'I want you to have all the information you need when you make your decision to work with me.'

She was confident and she had reason to be; she had a strong hand.

'What exactly would you want?'

'Oliver Spenser is dead. I want the four agents who were responsible for the murder of my husband and the abduction of my little girl. Their names are Lydia Chisholm, Connor English, Joshua Joyce and Bryan Duffy. Chisolm might be dead.'

'Why's that?'

'I stabbed her in the throat.'

'I see.'

'If she *is* dead, I want solid proof of it. The other three are out there somewhere. I want GCHQ to make finding them a top priority, and then I want you to pass me the information. I'll take care of what happens after that.'

'But we wouldn't have to worry about them?'

'They'll go quiet. You wouldn't have to worry about them.'

A car went by, sweeping its headlights into the cabin and, for a moment, he saw her hard, implacable face. 'No,' he said. 'I don't think we would.'

'And most of all I want Control.'

'That's five,' Pope said. 'How are you going to get all of them?'

'One at a time.' He heard the door open. 'I'm going to get out of the car now. I'm not unreasonable. I know you'll have to give this some thought.'

'I'll need a couple of days.'

'You can have a week. I'm not going anywhere.'

'How will I find you?'

'You won't,' she said. 'I'll find you.'

Beatrix Rose stepped out of the car. Pope found he had been holding his breath. He looked in the wing mirror and watched as she stepped between the two cars parked behind him, turned to the left, and then disappeared. He stayed where he was for a long minute, staring into the dark and watching the lights of the stacked planes as they patiently waited for their chance to land. She was a dangerous woman, he knew that much for sure. Dangerous didn't even cover it. Years of enforced exile would have filled her to the brim with spite and bitterness and there was no telling what consequences that might have.

How reliable was she? How much could he trust her?

She did have a point, though: he had no idea about any of the men and women that had been bequeathed to him. Were there any bad apples? Which ones? Were they all bad apples? And she had the evidence of Control's corruption. It was difficult to imagine how deep down the rabbit hole that would go.

He heard the sound of a high-performance motorcycle engine somewhere behind the car. A single high-beam headlight cut through the dusk and a red, white and green Ducati 1098 roared by the outside of the car. The engine growled and the rear light cluster glowed red as the rider braked at the exit and then, as the gate lifted, the engine howled again as the rider fed revs and accelerated onto the road and away.

Pope shook his head. The way he saw it, he really didn't have any choice. If he didn't take up Rose's offer, she would probably find them all herself. It would just take a little longer. In the meantime, she could bring down British intelligence. Didn't it make better sense to take advantage of the very particular set of skills that she could bring to the table?

Pope started his car and pulled away.

The motorcycle was already long gone.

59

Milton smiled at the steward and handed him his boarding card. The man checked it and smiled in return, welcoming him on board and directing him down to the right, into economy. He had a window seat just in front of the wing. He nodded at the woman sitting in the aisle and she unclipped her belt and stood so that he could sit. He sat down and stuffed the copy of *Great Expectations* that he had bought in the airport shop into the mesh pouch on the back of the seat in front of him. Space was a little tight and his knees bumped up against the seat. He looked out of the window at the runway and the terminal buildings beyond. The headlights of the service vehicles that buzzed around the big jet raked across the runway.

The woman next to him bumped her elbow against his as she gripped his armrest by mistake.

'I'm sorry,' the woman next to him said. 'My nerves are awful. I'm a terrible flyer.'

'Quite all right,' Milton said.

She was quiet as the plane rolled down the taxiway, following the queue of jets waiting for their take-off slots. As they swung around at the end of the approach, perpendicular to the start of the runway, the angle allowed them to watch the BA flight ahead of them as its engines boomed and it climbed slowly into the air.

'I hate take-off the worst of all,' the woman said. Her face was a little pale.

Milton gave her his most reassuring smile. 'You probably know the statistics. You were more likely to get into a situation on the way to the airport than you are now.'

'Thanks,' she said.

Milton smiled, but said nothing.

'I'm Sadie.'

Milton didn't really want to get into a conversation; he would have preferred to read his book for an hour or two and then try to catch some sleep. 'I'm John.'

'Is this business or pleasure?'

He thought about that; it was an excellent question.

'A bit of both.'

'What do you do?'

'I'm between jobs.'

She carried on talking, vague sentences tumbling out with nervous energy.

Milton kept an open, friendly expression to his face and made the appropriate responses when they were required, but he quickly zoned her out. This was business, not pleasure. He had been unable to decide upon his destination after Pope left and so he had bought a newspaper and a sandwich and found an empty seat. He had opened the newspaper and started to read, trusting that something would present itself. The story that had finally caught his eye was on the tenth page, buried in the international news. It had snagged his attention and, no matter how much he tried to think about something else, he could not. He'd made up his mind. He had finished the sandwich and went to buy a one-way ticket from the desk.

The pilot jockeyed the jumbo around until it was on the runway, nose pointing straight down the centre line. The engines cycled up and the jet lurched forwards. The woman stopped speaking, gripping her armrests so hard that her knuckles showed white through the skin on the back of her hands.

Milton looked out of the window as they sped past the buildings, the lights merging into a multicoloured blur. They roared past the terminal and out the other side and the cabin tilted gently as the jet took to the air. Front wheels, back wheels, and up. Milton kept watching as the airport opened up beneath them, and then the lights of the towns and villages that surrounded it, the cars on the motorway, the late-night train that snaked its way east towards London.

He looked down on England and wondered when he would see it again.

Perhaps he never would.

John Milton closed his eyes and thought about what he was going to do next.

MARK DAWSON is the bestselling author of the Beatrix Rose, Isabella Rose and John Milton series and has sold over four million books. He lives in Wiltshire with his family and can be reached at www.markjdawson.com

www.facebook.com/markdawsonauthor
www.twitter.com/pbackwriter
www.instagram.com.markjdawson

Get Exclusive John Milton Material

Building a relationship with my readers is the very best thing about writing. Join my VIP Reader Club for information on new books and a copy of Milton's battle with the Mafia and an assassin called Tarantula.

You can get your content **for free,** by signing up at my website.

Just visit www.markjdawson.com.

WELBECK

PUBLISHING GROUP

Love books? Join the club.

Sign up and choose your preferred genres to receive tailored news, deals, extracts, author interviews and more about your next favourite read.

From heart-racing thrillers to award-winning historical fiction, through to must-read music tomes, beautiful picture books and delightful gift ideas, Welbeck is proud to publish titles that suit every taste.

bit.ly/welbeckpublishing

WELBECK

ANDRE DEUTSCH

MORTIMER

MORTIMER

WELBECK